Rascal
DOES NOT DREAM
of a
Sister
Home
Alone

HAJIME
KAMOSHIDA

Illustration by
KEJI MIZOGUCHI

Rascal
DOES NOT DREAM
of a
Sister
Home
Alne

HAJIME KAMOSHIDA

Illustration by
KEJI MIZOGUCHI

YEN
ON

New York

Rascal Does Not Dream of a Sister Home Alone
Hajime Kamoshida

Translation by Andrew Cunningham
Cover art by Keji Mizoguchi

SEISHUN BUTA YARO WA ORUSUBAN IMOTO NO YUME WO MINAI Vol. 5
©Hajime Kamoshida 2015
Edited by Dengeki Bunko
First published in Japan in 2015 by KADOKAWA CORPORATION, Tokyo.
English translation rights arranged with KADOKAWA CORPORATION, Tokyo through
TUTTLE-MORI AGENCY, INC., Tokyo.

English translation © 2021 by Yen Press, LLC

Yen On
150 West 30th Street, 19th Floor
New York, NY 10001

Visit us at yenpress.com
facebook.com/yenpress
twitter.com/yenpress
yenpress.tumblr.com
instagram.com/yenpress

First Yen On Edition: July 2021

Yen On is an imprint of Yen Press, LLC.
The Yen On name and logo are trademarks of Yen Press, LLC.

Library of Congress Cataloging-in-Publication Data
Names: Kamoshida, Hajime, 1978– author. | Mizoguchi, Keji, illustrator.
Title: Rascal does not dream of bunny girl senpai / Hajime Kamoshida ;
illustration by Keji Mizoguchi.
Other titles: Seishun buta yarō. English
Description: New York, NY : Yen On, 2020. |
Contents: v. 1. Rascal does not dream of bunny girl senpai —
v. 2. Rascal does not dream of petite devil kohai —
v. 3. Rascal does not dream of logical witch —
v. 4. Rascal does not dream of siscon idol —
v. 5. Rascal does not dream of a sister home alone
Identifiers: LCCN 2020004455 | ISBN 9781975399351 (v. 1 ; trade paperback) |
ISBN 9781975312541 (v. 2 ; trade paperback) | ISBN 9781975312565 (v. 3 ; trade paperback) |
ISBN 9781975312589 (v. 4 ; trade paperback) | ISBN 9781975312602 (v. 5 ; trade paperback)
Subjects: CYAC: Fantasy.
Classification: LCC PZ7.1.K218 Ras 2020 | DDC [Fic]—dc23
LC record available at https://lccn.loc.gov/2020004455

ISBNs: 978-1-9753-1260-2 (paperback)
978-1-9753-1261-9 (ebook)

3 5 7 9 10 8 6 4 2

TPA

Printed in South Korea

To: Sakuta

Can we meet at the beach at Shichirigahama tomorrow?

Shouko

Chapter
1

the rest of that day
is today

1

Sakuta Azusagawa had been worried all morning.

The reason for this was a letter that had arrived in his mailbox the day before.

The letter was from "Shouko."

For a long time, that name had brought back painful memories. But lately, it had taken on other meanings.

Now, when he heard the name, two people came to mind. Or rather—the original had been joined by a second.

This new Shouko Makinohara was a first-year junior high school student he'd met about three months ago. She was a sweet-natured, earnest, adorable little girl.

The other was a high school girl who existed only in his memories. He'd met that Shouko Makinohara when he was in his third year of junior high. Two years had passed since they last spoke on the beach at Shichirigahama, and he'd been unable to locate her again. If she had continued with her education as expected, she'd be a college freshman now.

Something about the tone of this letter sounded more like the latter, older Shouko.

He'd called the younger one's cell phone the day before, just to be sure, but it had gone to her voice mail. Rather than ask about the letter there, he'd left a message saying he'd call back and hung up.

There was still no word from her, so the letter remained a mystery. And his mind was still going in circles.

The best way to clear this all up was to follow the instructions. Go to the beach at Shichirigahama and see which Shouko was there. Talking to Shouko directly would at least get him somewhere.

He'd reached that conclusion the night before.

The problem was what came next.

If the letter was from the Shouko he'd met two years ago, that meant it was from his first love.

Should he really just show up to meet her?

After all, he was dating someone else now.

He felt like he should talk to his girlfriend first, but maybe it wouldn't make a difference.

No matter how he framed it, he was in a relationship and would be going to see his first love again.

He sighed, unable to find a way out of this thought loop.

"Ow!"

A sharp pain shot through his foot. He looked down. A leg clad in black tights was extended in his direction, perfectly positioned to drive the heel of a shoe into his foot.

A slim, beautiful leg. He drank in the sight of it a moment before following it upward to the lovely face of the girl it belonged to.

"What's wrong?" she asked, smiling at him.

Mai was leaning against the doors of the train. Mai Sakurajima. She was a year older than Sakuta, a third-year student. An actress famous nationwide, she was also his girlfriend.

She was unusually tall, with jet-black hair that had never once been dyed. Intelligent eyes. Everything about her was mature, lending her a composure beyond her years.

Her standing here in the doorway, with a view of the sea visible through the windows behind her—that alone was a work of art.

She had the kind of beauty other girls aspired to. The news last night had reported the results of a poll on "Who high school girls most want to look like," and Mai had won by a landslide.

Why was someone that popular stepping on his foot with a pleasant smile?

"Mai, what am I being punished for?"

"You're with me but acting all out of it."

"That's just how I seem most of the time."

"Then what was I talking about?"

She seemed pretty sure he wouldn't know.

"Uh…we're on a Type 10 train today?"

There were several kinds of trains running on the Enoden line between Fujisawa Station and Kamakura Station. The Type 10 was a distinctively old-fashioned, fancy-looking car, kinda like the Orient Express. It had an iconic dark-blue base with a white stripe running around the windows. The interiors featured striking woodwork, giving it a touch of class and elegance.

"Nobody was talking about trains."

Her tone didn't change, but her gaze turned frosty.

"Uh, then…"

"Joking isn't gonna let you wriggle out of this one," she said, rounding on him.

"Sorry," he said, unsure what other options he had left.

"*Sigh…*"

His ears stung. She gave him a look that was half pity, half aggravation.

"I was thanking you for yesterday."

"Yesterday?"

"For helping Nodoka move in."

"Oh."

"And to return the favor, I said I'd come over to make dinner tonight."

As she said this, her eyes shifted downward. A tinge of

embarrassment. Her lips twisted slightly, as if annoyed he'd forced her to say it twice.

"Toyohama doesn't need to eat?"

Nodoka Toyohama was Mai's sister from a different mother. After a long and complicated series of events, they'd decided to live together.

"She'll be back late from her lessons, so she'll be eating with the rest of her group."

"Ah."

Nodoka was part of a relatively new idol group, Sweet Bullet. They had song and dance lessons every day and traveled a lot on weekends, doing short concerts. Nodoka was nowhere near as famous as Mai, but when he'd teased her about that, she'd sworn to become so famous he would have to eat his words. Sakuta was looking forward to it.

"You're acting weird today," Mai said, watching his expression closely.

"Oh? How so?"

"I'm gonna cook for you, but you don't even crack a smile? I expected more."

She sounded disgruntled.

"No, I'm happy. It's just…we're on the train."

There were people watching. Now that Mai was back to work, she attracted a lot of attention. Even on their regular morning commute to school.

"Hmph. Fine, I'll let you have this one."

But she didn't take her eyes off him. Clearly not the least bit convinced. But she wiped the look of discontent off her face and asked, "What's in your fridge?"

"Haven't gone shopping yet, so it's nearly empty."

"Then we'll have to hit a store on the way home."

"Uh…I hate to admit this now, but I've got plans after school…"

"I thought you didn't have a shift today, though."

"It's not work related."

It was the letter.

The invitation hadn't specified a time, but since it was a weekday...right after school seemed the logical choice. He didn't think anyone would expect him to show up at five AM, and he couldn't exactly walk around the beach while school was in session. That was true for "Shouko" as well.

"Then what?" Mai asked.

"Just a thing."

"A thing?"

"Not important."

"Riiight."

She backed off but kept her eyes glued to him.

It would be weirder if she'd bought that one. He hadn't exactly found a convincing excuse.

"You don't have to tell me if you don't want to."

"I'm not trying to be secretive, just..."

He meant what he said. He didn't want to keep the letter from her. He'd already told Mai about the Shouko from two years ago and his feelings for her, and how he'd only taken the exam and attended Minegahara High to see her again. She knew all of this. So there was nothing left to hide.

But when she'd asked him about it point-blank, Sakuta had tensed up. For some reason, he wasn't sure he should share this with her.

There was too much he didn't understand about the letter, and telling her about it now would just leave her with confusing information. He felt like it was better to say nothing.

But as he thought about that, their train reached the station.

Shichirigahama Station. The one closest to Minegahara High.

Rows of uniform-clad students filed out onto the tiny platform.

Each one ran their IC commuter pass through the simple, scarecrow-like gate as they exited.

Sakuta and Mai joined the flow of bodies and headed to the street outside.

The train had reached the station at exactly the right time to stop Mai from asking any follow-up questions.

They crossed a bridge and then a set of tracks.

And their school gates were right in front of them.

It felt like he'd safely gotten away.

He allowed himself to feel relieved.

The moment he did, Mai spoke again.

"I don't know what you're hiding, but it'll all come out in time, so you'd better have thought of a good excuse by then."

It was like he was a log, and she was hammering a metal spike into him.

This must have been what people meant by "struck speechless."

"You get it, right?" Mai said, like she was training a puppy.

"Yeah…," he said. That was the only option left open to him.

Sakuta spent his morning classes gazing absently out the window at the beach below. Thinking about what excuse he could give Mai. English, math, physics, and Japanese all ended with the teacher warning them that midterms were right around the corner and they should be ready, but this went in one ear and out the other.

Classes were the last thing on his mind. He had to come up with a way to tell her about the letter, and how to explain his failure to do so that morning. But ignoring his morning lessons hadn't gotten him any closer to a convincing reason.

This was still all he could think of when lunch rolled around.

Failing to make any headway, he ate quickly and left his classroom.

His destination was the science lab.

"Futaba, I'm coming in."

"Don't."

Sakuta ignored that, sliding the door open.

The room's sole occupant was a girl—his friend Rio Futaba. She was pretty small, only five foot one, and always wore a long white lab coat. Her hair was done up in the back, and she shot him a brief, annoyed look through her glasses.

Futaba was at the lab table by the blackboard. In front of her was a lit alcohol lamp, but instead of the usual beaker or test tube, she had a coffee siphon on it.

"What's with that?" Sakuta asked, pointing at the siphon. He took a seat across the table from her.

"I think the physics teacher brought it in."

"And you're using it without permission? You shock me sometimes."

"Having an accomplice eases my guilty conscience."

Was she roping him into this? He had other business today, so he let it pass without comment. Rio wasn't exactly trying to start a debate or anything, either. She'd most likely just meant it as an offhand comment.

"So, uh, Futaba…"

The boiling water in the siphon's lower section was rising into the vessel above via the principle of vapor pressure. He'd marveled at it the first time he saw it happen, and it was still fun to watch. As the water hit the ground coffee, a dark brown seeped into it.

"How many times does this make, Azusagawa?"

The look she gave him was beyond irritation or frustration. It was more like pity.

"This isn't about Adolescence Syndrome. Honest."

Rio looked surprised. Like she'd received the shock of her life.

"Though it might turn out to be related later…"

There was definitely a strong chance Adolescence Syndrome was behind the Shouko mystery. It certainly would explain a lot.

"Hmm."

Showing no more apparent interest, Rio removed the siphon from the alcohol lamp. She put the lid on and turned the flame off. After a minute, the coffee passed back through the filter into the round vessel below.

She poured half the coffee into her own mug and then the other half into a nearby beaker, which she placed in front of Sakuta.

He shot her a glance to confirm the beaker was safe. It was hard to not be at least slightly concerned it might've taken part in some weird experiment.

"I've only used it for a concentrated sodium chloride fusion experiment, so it should be fine."

"That is a terrifying combination of words."

"You know what sodium chloride is?"

"Salt, right?"

"Yep."

"Then say that."

"I boiled the beaker to sterilize it after. Don't worry."

When he was sure it was safe, he took a sip. Flavor and scent were both a significant step up from the instant stuff. It was much more coffee-like. It improved the entire science lab experience.

"So what's the matter, specifically?"

"I wanna ask you about this," Sakuta said. He took the letter out of his jacket pocket and handed it to her.

Seeing is believing.

"What is it?"

"A letter from 'Shouko.'"

"You're walking around with a letter from a girl in your pocket? That's just creepy."

With that brutal evaluation, she opened the envelope. Her eyes moved left to right, quickly reading it.

"Ah. That explains the scare quotes. This definitely doesn't read like something a junior high school girl would write. She would've addressed you more politely, too."

Rio had met the younger Shouko. Last summer, at Sakuta's house.

"And this 'tomorrow' is today?"

"I think so. I found it in my mailbox yesterday."

Rio carefully placed it back in the envelope and returned it to him.

"You told Sakurajima about it?"

That was the first thing she homed in on. Not anything about Shouko.

"No…"

"So you're asking me to help you cheat on her," Rio said flatly as she took a sip of coffee.

"I'm not. Stop getting weird ideas."

"Then why keep it from her?" she asked pointedly.

"What's the best way to tell her?" He pretended he hadn't heard her.

"You should have gone right to her yesterday, the moment you found the letter. If you'd consulted her while still visibly rattled, then you could've shared the problem."

That was a logical, exemplary answer. Very Rio-like.

She was right, of course. He couldn't argue with it at all. But unfortunately, that opportunity was long gone. It was already the next day. And he'd been super evasive about it on the train that morning, so Mai was well aware something was up.

"Futaba."

"What?"

"Why didn't you tell me that yesterday?"

"You didn't ask."

"I know."

"But it isn't like you to sweat this sort of thing."

"Really?"

"You usually just act like her being mad is a reward and tell her outright."

"What do you think I am?"

"A rascal who gets off on being insulted."

"……"

He shouldn't have asked.

"It kinda…just didn't feel fair."

"Fair?" Rio looked baffled. He'd lost her.

"If it was the other way around and Mai suddenly said, 'I'm going to see my first love today,' I know for a fact I wouldn't feel comfortable."

"You're confident about the weirdest things."

"But I wouldn't be able to tell her *not* to, and I wouldn't *want* to, so I'd just stew about it in private."

"So telling her would mean you'd get to feel better because you aren't keeping any secrets, but hearing all of this would force Sakurajima to bottle up her own feelings, and you don't want to do that to her."

"Basically."

"If this were a secret you could take to your grave, then maybe it would be better not to bother her with it. But…"

Rio trailed off into a meaningful look.

"But what?"

"Sakurajima doesn't think like that. She would want to be a character in this story. Or are you forgetting how she told everyone you were dating with the cameras rolling?"

That had happened recently. The first juicy gossip Mai Sakurajima had ever been involved with. Several people had taken pictures of Mai and Sakuta together and spread them online, at which point they'd been picked up by the weekly magazines—and then the whole country knew.

But Mai herself had silenced the uproar. The media had flocked to a press conference announcing production on a new movie, and she'd politely handled question after question, blushing as she told them about their relationship.

"That was the only way to handle it."

Nobody knew the truth—those photos had all been taken when Mai and Nodoka were in each other's bodies, thanks to a bout of Adolescence Syndrome. All the photos were of Nodoka, not Mai. Mai had dealt with the situation to keep Nodoka from feeling guilty.

"All the same, if there's a problem, she's the type of person who'll want to face it head-on."

"True."

Growing up in show business had been a harsh teacher, and it had made Mai strong.

"Especially if you're involved, Azusagawa."

"Apparently, she loves me more than I think."

"I wouldn't know…"

Rio sounded like she'd lost interest. The reason for that was in her hands. She was playing with her phone.

"What are you doing?"

Searching something online?

It wasn't often Rio messed with her phone during a conversation.

"I decided it would be faster to report all this directly to Sakurajima."

"Huh?"

He felt like he'd just received very bad news, but surely he was hearing things.

"She's on her way."

"What? Wait!"

Apparently, she was being serious.

"She gave me her number over the summer. While I was staying at your place…she said to text her if anything came up."

"First I've heard of it!"

Sakuta gave her a look of dismay, every inch of him radiating protest.

"Futaba!" he wailed, but that was all he got out before he heard footsteps in the hall.

They were instantly recognizable. Unhurried, elegant. He'd know them anywhere.

Sakuta spun around to face the door.

It slid open a second later.

Mai stood on the threshold.

"Enjoy," Rio said and rose to leave.

"Traitor!" Sakuta yelled. Rio didn't even flinch.

"Thank you, Futaba."

"Not at all."

Rio bobbed her head as they passed each other in the doorway, and then she left without looking back.

He heard her walk off down the hall. When they were out of earshot, Mai stepped inside, closing the door firmly behind her.

".......,"

".......,"

Their eyes had been locked on each other since Mai's arrival. Sakuta felt like breaking eye contact would just make her mad.

"Sakuta."

"Yes, what is it?"

It was just the two of them. But the science lab was crackling with tension.

"Will you be back by six?"

He'd assumed she would yell at him, but her tone was downright gentle.

"Huh?" He blinked at her, not sure what she meant.

"I told you this morning I'm coming over to cook."

"Oh, right. Yeah, I think I can make it."

He didn't know why "Shouko" had sent him the letter, but if Mai was saying he had to be back by six, Sakuta would do whatever was necessary to make that happen.

But he didn't get what she was thinking. What did this mean?

"Then I'll be over around that time."

"Okay."

"……"

"……"

He waited a bit, but Mai said nothing else. Like that was all she wanted to say.

"Uh, Mai…is that it?"

"You want me to be jealous?"

"Well, maybe a little. Mostly…are we good?"

He picked his words carefully, watching her expression.

Mai continued smiling as she stepped closer to him.

"Of course not," she said and twisted his cheek.

"Ow…"

"My boyfriend's going to meet his old flame? And that's more important than my invitation? What could possibly be good about that?"

"Right, sorry. Not good at owww."

"So you don't deny she's an old flame."

"No, no, I explained our relationship. It never got that far."

"I know," she said, rolling her eyes. Her hand was still firmly twisting his cheek. "And that's why I tried to let you go see her without another word. But you just haaad to ask."

"It was tactless of me, I admit."

"And…oh, what's the right word? I'm…curious what her deal is, too. And what connection the two Shoukos have."

"Makes sense."

Sakuta had spent a lot of time on that himself. Ever since he met the younger Shouko, really. He was sure they were the same person, but that was also ostensibly impossible.

If he met the Shouko behind this letter, maybe he'd learn something. He hoped he would anyway.

"So that's why you're okay with it."

"Also because I can tell you still have feelings for her."

She sounded awfully certain about that.

"Come again?"

"You have feelings for Shouko."

"Noooo. I really don't."

He *had* taken the Minegahara entrance exam hoping to see her again. It was also true he'd been in love with her. But the bulk of his heart was now filled with Mai. That fact was unassailable.

"Not, like, *those* kinds of feelings. But two years ago, when you hit rock bottom, she was the one who helped you."

"That's…true, sure."

If he hadn't met Shouko, his current life probably would've been unrecognizable. She'd had that much impact on him. But he'd never thanked her properly for it. By the time he realized how much she'd done for him, he'd already lost contact with her.

She'd left him with no closure, no time to sort his feelings out, no indication this would be the last time they'd see each other. It had never occurred to him she'd just vanish. He'd been so sure they'd meet again, he'd even said "See you later" as they parted.

Mai's fingers finally loosened their grip on Sakuta's cheek.

"It's all red," she said, gently rubbing it. "I don't want you to carry this emotional baggage if you don't have to. You've finally got a chance, so I want you to do this right."

Sakura felt like she'd loaded a lot of meaning into the word *right*. But he didn't stop to go through the list. He didn't need to do that to understand her feelings. And he was her boyfriend. He wanted to do "right" by those feelings. Failing to do that would just be sad.

She'd let him off the hook, but he was still utterly defeated.

She'd approached the issue with real maturity and left him in awe.

"What do you say?"

Mai flashed him a confident smile. There was a mischievous edge to it that suggested she knew full well this had made him fall even more in love with her.

Unwilling to admit defeat, he ignored her question and turned away.

"Sakuta?"

Ignoring this, too, he strode to the windows and flung one open.

Then he took a deep breath.

"I love you, Maiiiii!"

His voice echoed across the grounds.

"Er, Sakuta?!" For once, she actually sounded panicked.

"I love youuuuuuu! Ow."

Someone had slapped the back of his head.

Pretending like it hurt, he turned around to find Mai glaring at him, half aggravated, half embarrassed.

"Stop. It's embarrassing."

"I feel like I had to do it this way for you to understand."

"It's obnoxious."

"Aww."

"Find another way to express yourself."

She stuck her lips out, pouting.

"Er, um…"

He put his hands on her shoulders and moved his face closer to hers. Her hand shot up between them and pushed his face back. Hard.

"Owww."

A brutal rejection.

"But why?"

"You do *not* get to kiss me when you're about to go see your old flame."

"I thought you just said it was okay."

"You can meet her, but that doesn't mean I have to *like* it."

When she put it that way, it was kinda obvious, really. Logically and practically, she was allowing him to meet Shouko. But that didn't mean her emotions fell in line. There was no shortage of things in life that were unpleasant but nonetheless necessary. And this was one of them.

"So you'd better put in the work to get back on my good side before I let you do anything like *that*."

She made a show of being all grumpy.

Maybe he should buy her a pudding on the way home.

That always worked with his sister, Kaede. If he got the good pudding, any bad mood would dissipate in no time. It was like a magic item.

"And just to be clear, pudding won't solve this one."

Her eyes saw right through him.

"Er, so…what would?"

"You need to figure that out yourself. Your homework, due by dinner tonight."

"Aww."

He tried to grumble like usual, but it came out a bit screechier than usual. Mai looked thoroughly satisfied.

2

Sakuta spent the afternoon classes once more not listening to his teachers. Instead, he was working on the homework Mai had assigned him. It involved only one question.

Q: How to get back on Mai's good side?

This was a very thorny problem. Harder than anything on the entrance exams at the nation's top universities.

Normally, he could just say how he felt, and that would wear her

down. That didn't seem likely to work this time. Shouting at the school yard hadn't worked, either. It seemed doubtful that words alone would do the trick.

Should he change tactics and get her some sort of gift? No, that would just make her mad at him. "Don't try to buy your way out of this" or the like. And he had no idea what kind of present would get him anywhere with her. She was a famous actress. If she wanted something, she could just purchase it herself.

He was getting nowhere.

"Uh-oh…"

Was it just his imagination, or was making him sweat like this already a pretty significant punishment? Had Mai assigned him this homework knowing it'd turn out like this?

It was certainly effective. He hadn't thought about anything but her all afternoon. Technically, this morning had been the same— he'd really been thinking about her the whole time.

And yet the bell rang and classes ended without him arriving at any real answer.

The final homeroom was quickly over, and it was time to leave.

Sakuta picked up his bag and left his seat. He headed for the hall, still racking his brain.

As he stepped through the door, he nearly walked right into someone very tall.

"Whoops, sorry… Wait, Sakuta?"

He looked up and saw his friend Yuuma Kunimi.

"Oh, Kunimi."

It was mid-October, but Yuuma still had a tan. He was wearing a tracksuit with *Minegahara High Basketball* embroidered on it.

"Practice again?"

"Like basically every day, yeah."

Yuuma worked at the same restaurant as Sakuta, pulling nearly as many shifts despite all the basketball practice. Where did he get the energy?

They headed down the hall together. They were going different places, but to get to the gym or the front doors, the same stairs were needed.

"Hey, Kunimi…"

"Mm?"

"How do you get back on a girl's good side?"

"Huh? What'd you do this time?" Yuuma chuckled. "Fighting with Sakurajima? Just say you're sorry."

Why did he look so pleased?

"Kunimi, you've fought with your girlfriend before, right? I'd bet you have. Especially with that personality of hers."

Yuuma was dating a second-year girl from their school, a classmate of Sakuta's. Her name was Saki Kamisato. Supposedly the cutest girl in her year, she was the leader of the popular girl clique in his class. Which made her the de facto leader of all the girls. He wasn't sure if that was the source of her pride, but she had it in for Sakuta—a perennial outcast. She'd gone so far as to order him not to speak to Yuuma. That had been quite a shock.

Her mean streak had to come out from time to time when she was with Yuuma as well. It wouldn't be fair if it didn't.

"And what kind of personality is that?"

"She's a lovely girl who's very willing to share her sense of righteousness with me."

"She doesn't beat around the bush, that's for sure."

Yuuma knew exactly what Sakuta meant, but he always did this. Deliberately twisted things around into something positive. Never had a bad thing to say about her.

"To be fair, I get on her bad side often enough."

Yuuma winced a bit at the memory.

"How do you fix that?"

"I don't do anything special."

"Your 'nothing special' is probably something ridiculously cool, so just tell me already."

"You have way too high an opinion of me. It really isn't anything special. I just use the message function on a free communication app to send her a funny-looking sticker."

"You what?"

"We send those back and forth for a bit, and before you know it, we've laughed it off."

"And you're telling me this out of sheer spite, since you know I don't have a phone?"

"Look, it's the answer to the question you asked."

As they headed down the stairs, they passed some first-years. Yuuma waved at them.

"Anything else?"

"Take her on a date somewhere she mentioned wanting to go."

"Hmm."

"Get her something she's said she wanted."

"And?"

"Uh, she really likes that Gaburincho Bear character, so I buy that merch for her. That's it."

"You've got it rough, huh?"

That was more answers than he'd expected. Sakuta gave him a look of pity.

"Never feels like that when it's your girlfriend, though."

"That sounds impressive but destroys all sympathy I might have had for you."

"Whoa, *you're* the one who made me say all this," Yuuma complained, but he sounded happy.

"But I think it helped. Thanks."

"Cool. Gotta leave you here."

They were almost at the front doors, so Yuuma waved a hand and jogged off down the covered walkway to the gym.

Sakuta watched him go and then started working through the received advice.

He was soon at an impasse.

"Places she wants to go? Things she wants? Mai never mentions anything like that."

He was stuck again.

Despite finally getting some practical advice, it wasn't helping. He would have to coax information out of her, but this was Mai. If he started asking indirect questions, she'd know what he was up to instantly. And that would just force him further into the corner.

He had to think of another approach.

By now he was standing at his shoe locker. He changed into his shoes, put his slippers away, and then sensed something wrong.

"Yikes, I've gotta take a shit."

And not just any shit. This was an urgent call. Almost certainly caused by stress. But if he stopped at the bathroom and missed Shouko, all this worrying would be for nothing.

Hoping the urge would pass in time, he headed outside.

He was walking a little faster than usual. Quickly passing the other students.

The gate was coming up quick. Beyond that was the crossing, yellow-and-black-striped poles standing upright, reaching for the sky.

He saw this every day. The students walking around him all took this path on a daily basis, too. But as he neared the school gates, he sensed something different. The students ahead of him were all *noticing* something.

As Sakuta neared the gate, he saw a girl with her back to him, stopped in her tracks. Long hair swaying in the wind. He recognized her instantly. It was Mai.

"Mai, what's up?" he asked. He couldn't just breeze on by.

"Oh, Sakuta," she said, turning back. "Perfect timing. This girl wants a word with you."

Mai was facing someone by the side of the gates. She wore the uniform from another school and glasses. This girl was noticeably younger than them, with a bit of a baby face. He took another look and thought her sailor uniform seemed familiar.

"……"

He might be imagining it, but…before they'd moved to Fujisawa, Sakuta had lived in Yokohama. And this resembled his junior high uniform to an uncanny degree. He plucked the thread from a sea of memories and felt like it had something on the end of it. A catch.

"You want to talk to me?" he asked, hoping to find out what that might be.

"Yes. You're Kae's brother, right?"

He recognized that wording, too. Only one person had ever called him "Kae's brother."

"Do you remember me? We used to live in the same building. I lived upstairs. Kotomi Kano."

He finally placed her just as she said her name.

"…I only just remembered, sorry."

She was someone they'd known before moving to Fujisawa. A neighbor from back in Yokohama. And she'd been friends with Kaede.

"So, um…" Kotomi was fidgeting, glancing at the crowds.

They were right by the gates, and tons of students were flowing out. Wearing a different uniform alone made her stand out, but she was talking to Mai, a nationally famous actress, and Sakuta, a well-known figure of ill repute in this school. Stares were unavoidable.

A few people were even sniggering. This was more likely because they'd heard him yelling out the window earlier, but Kotomi had no way of knowing that, and she flinched visibly.

"Sakuta, maybe take this somewhere else?" Mai suggested.

"Good…idea," he said, but he offered no suggestion. It was a clear sign this situation had put him off-balance. He hadn't expected to meet anyone from the past like this. It had never even occurred to him that someone might try to get in touch.

"Er, um...I'm sorry. I shouldn't have just shown up like this."

"No, that's not a problem at all."

His head was finally starting to work. What now? If she'd come all this way, she must have had a reason for it, so he couldn't just send her packing. For a junior high school student, taking several trains to the next city over was a pretty big adventure. He didn't want to brush off the courage residing in that tiny frame. Especially if this was connected to Kaede.

"Uh, Mai, I hate to say it, but..."

He could only think of one solution.

"I get it. I'll run down to the beach," she sighed, jumping ahead of him. "I'll recognize her if I know the younger one?"

"Her" being the older Shouko.

"I think so, yeah."

He was already having second thoughts about asking her to handle this. It felt like he'd just turned the dial on life straight to the danger zone.

But that didn't mean he could just ditch Kotomi here, and it would be weird to drag her along to the meeting, too.

"The situation demands it," Mai said matter-of-factly.

She'd clearly gotten an urgent vibe from Kotomi's demeanor, too. Mai had gained a grim set to her jaw, too.

"Come get me when you're done," she said and walked away.

The students were all turning right, headed for the station. Mai went the other way, toward the water.

——*"The situation demands it."*

Mai was right about that.

He took a deep breath and turned back to Kotomi.

"This way," he said.

* * *

"Welcome!" the girl at the register said brightly as Sakuta and Kotomi Kano stepped inside.

This was a fast-food place a five-minute walk from Minegahara High.

Half the seats were full. A lazy afternoon vibe permeated the interior.

He led Kotomi to an empty seat by the windows overlooking the water and sat down opposite her. This was a chain shop that could be found everywhere, but with a view like this, it felt much grander.

That feeling hit everyone their first time here. Kotomi was no exception. Nervous as she was, she still gaped at the view and said, "Wow!"

The price tags were the same as every other shop in the chain, so the food felt like a real bargain. Sadly, there was a sign on the door saying they would be closing at the end of the month.

An employee brought them some orange juice and took the number tag away. Kotomi straightened up and inserted her straw.

Before taking a sip, she said, "I'm sorry to just show up like this. Was I interrupting something?"

"It's taken care of."

It really wasn't, and Sakuta was actually dreading going to the beach after this, but at this point, he had to just accept his fate. Giving up was vital to life.

"Sorry," she said again.

He remembered her being a smart kid. They'd known her since kindergarten, and Kotomi always had it together. Always a few steps ahead of the other kids her age. Meanwhile, Kaede had lagged behind the others. Kotomi had spent a lot of time helping her.

Like, Kaede always took her time eating, so Kotomi would wait for her. And she was a slow runner, so Kotomi would take her hand and pull her along.

Since she lived upstairs from them, she and Kaede had played together nearly every day.

They shared a class for all six years of grade school.

But in junior high, they'd been split up.

Even so, for the first month, they'd walked to school together.

Things started to change after Golden Week. They both started spending more time with friends from their new classes, and he didn't see them together as much. Kotomi didn't come over any more.

That was the last memory he had of her.

She hadn't worn glasses back then and had been more childish than she was now. Her features had certainly sharpened since.

"Oh, the glasses?" she said, catching his look. She took them off, looking sheepish. "I can't really do contacts. I try to put them in, but my eyes just snap shut…"

She mimed applying contacts.

Kotomi had always seemed like the type of girl who could do anything, but even she had her weaknesses. You never really know people as well as you think.

Which was why he had no idea what brought Kotomi here now.

"So why come around now?" he asked. Figuring it was best to be direct. "And why here?"

When they'd moved to Fujisawa, he hadn't told anyone where they were going. The bullying had left Kaede deeply traumatized, and she needed to live somewhere where they didn't know anyone.

"I…I tried to forget," Kotomi said, staring at the crumpled straw wrapper. "All those awful things happened to Kae, and I couldn't do anything. And then the two of you moved away…"

"……"

"Everything they'd done to her came out. The faculty and board of education and…I don't even know who else. All these adults showed up, and…and then the girls who'd been mean to Kae started getting bullied by everybody else. People told them to die or drop out, or posted about it…until they all stopped coming to school as well."

"…Oh."

That was news to him. He'd avoided even thinking about his old neighborhood since the move. And when he'd tossed his phone into the ocean, he'd cut off all contact with his old life.

"When the last of them were gone, people acted like they'd banished the evil villains. Like it was over. Nobody ever mentioned Kae. It became, like, an unwritten rule that you could never talk about any of it."

"Is that why you tried to forget?"

"Sorry."

"I'm not criticizing you. And you've got nothing to apologize for, Kano. You weren't part of the crowd that was mean to Kaede."

"But I didn't do anything to stop them. While they were bullying Kae, all I did was sit in the next class and worry about her."

"Well, yeah. It wasn't your class. What could you have done?"

Class divides were huge within most schools. They were like giant invisible walls. Entering the wrong class was like walking on needles, even if you weren't doing anything wrong. Nobody would welcome an outsider from another class barging in.

If Kotomi had tried to openly support Kaede, it probably would've made the bullying worse. Kaede would have been blamed for violating those unwritten social rules.

"But even after Kae moved, I did nothing. I avoided ever mentioning her and actively tried to forget her. It got so I could barely breathe…"

Kotomi put her hand on her chest, like she was in genuine agony.

"And then I saw the stories about Mai Sakurajima."

Kotomi finally looked directly at Sakuta.

"You did?"

It took him a moment to work out why her name had come up.

"I saw the photos online—and thought, 'Wow, the boy she's with looks a lot like Kae's brother.'"

The photos in the weekly magazines were properly blurred out, but that wasn't true online. They were mostly taken from quite a distance, but someone who knew Sakuta personally could probably tell it was him. And there were quite a few pictures like that. They were probably—no, definitely still out there.

"So I looked into it more, digging deeper, and found a site that said Mai Sakurajima went to this school. I thought if I came here, I might find you. Once I made it that far, I just had to come."

She'd waited at the gate, found Mai, and called out to her. And Sakuta had come by a minute later.

"Um…is Kae doing all right?"

"She is. She loves staying home so much, she can't leave."

Kotomi looked unsure if this was good news or not.

"She really is doing all right," he said. "No reason for you to beat yourself up."

"Okay…"

"Is that all you wanted to know?"

"No," she said, hesitantly shaking her head. "Here."

Kotomi pulled a book out of her bag. A hardcover novel. The title was *The Prince Gave Me a Poisoned Apple*.

"I borrowed this from Kae but never got a chance to give it back."

He took the book from her and flipped through it. She'd taken good care of it. Probably because she planned to return it one day.

"Um."

"Mm?"

He slowly closed the book.

"Is there any way I could see her?"

Sakuta had been waiting for that question. But that was exactly why he made a show of thinking about it before turning his gaze to the ocean and saying, "I think it's better you don't."

"……"

"It would probably be a bit of a shock."

"…Of course. I imagine it would…bring back some painful memories."

Sakuta had meant Kotomi would be shocked, but he decided this interpretation worked just as well, so he didn't correct her.

"I'm sorry," she said. "I'm only thinking about myself again."

"Kano, if you could see Kaede, what then?"

"Huh?"

"Do you know what you'd say?"

She thought about that for a moment. "No," she said, hanging her head.

"Then you should at least figure that out first."

"……"

"Maybe if you met, the words would come naturally, but…I kinda suspect they wouldn't."

This was a bit presumptuous of him. But he was pretty sure he was right. And that was why he felt the need to tell her.

"Um."

"Mm?"

"Can I at least get your number?"

She pulled a phone out of her bag. The case had a panda pattern on it.

"Oh, sorry. I don't have a phone."

"Huh?"

She looked up like she couldn't believe her ears.

"Phones cause problems for Kaede."

"Oh…"

Kotomi knew enough to get what that meant. Kaede flinched any time she heard a ringtone or even the sound of a phone vibrating. An unmistakable expression of fear.

"Th-then I'll just leave you with my number," she said, opening her school bag. She took out a loose-leaf notebook, neatly tore off a corner, and wrote eleven digits on it.

She held it out to him.

"I don't know what I'd say if I met Kae now. But I'd like to talk about novels with her again someday."

"Okay. Thanks."

He hoped that day would come. He really did. It was getting hard to even imagine Kaede chatting happily with friends.

If today was the first step back to that, he was all for it. With that in mind, he took the scrap of paper with Kotomi's number.

Done talking, they downed their orange juice and left the shop.

They headed toward Shichirigahama Station. He was walking Kotomi back there.

Neither spoke on the way. Kotomi seemed lost in thought, so Sakuta left her to it.

"Um, I have something I'd like to ask…"

She only spoke up when they were already on the platform, waiting for her train.

"What is it?"

"Do you mind if I hold on to that book a little while longer?"

"……"

He didn't answer right away. He had a hunch why Kotomi had brought the book with her. And it definitely wasn't dutifully following the rules she'd been taught as a kid about making sure to give things back if you borrowed them.

Kotomi had said it herself.

She was trying to forget.

But she hadn't been able to.

How could she forget when a book of Kaede's was sitting right there, in her own bedroom? Any time she looked at it, all those memories came rushing back.

Which was exactly why Kotomi had come to see Sakuta. That explained everything.

"If it's weighing on your mind, I'd say you should let it go," he said, eyes glued to the tracks. Choices like that were necessary, sometimes. "Always trying to do the right thing really takes a lot out of you."

"...Yeah, I know," Kotomi whispered.

"But knowing that, if you choose to return the book yourself, Kano, I'm certainly not gonna stop you."

"Right."

"There's just no guarantee everything'll wrap up neatly, or that the day will ever come."

".....．"

This made her think for a while. One look at her face made it clear she was wavering. Half of her wanted to let the book go and take the easy way out. The other half wanted to hang on to it and hope for a beautiful resolution. These two urges were fighting for dominance within her.

Which was exactly why Sakuta took the book out of his bag. He thought the fact that she hesitated at all meant it was worth preserving her connection to Kaede.

".....．"

Kotomi's eyes locked onto the book's cover. Sakuta read the title again. *The Prince Gave Me a Poisoned Apple.* This book was definitely a poisoned apple for Kotomi. And it could well turn out to be one for Kaede, too.

Kotomi's hand slowly reached out and took the book. Her fingertips hadn't stopped trembling.

But when the train stopped at the platform, her grip tightened, and she pulled the book to her chest.

She thanked Sakuta again and got on the train.

"Be safe getting home."

"I will."

The doors slowly closed.

As the train pulled out, Kotomi bowed her head again. Sakuta raised a hand in acknowledgement. And then Kotomi's train left the station, bound for Kamakura.

Sakuta took his own leave and headed toward the beach.

They'd been talking for a while, so the sun was hanging low in the west, preparing to set behind Enoshima.

He reached Route 134, waited for the light, and crossed. There was a set of stairs leading down to the beach at the end of the crosswalk. He took it one step at a time. Oddly enough, he didn't feel tense at all.

He stepped off the last stair onto the loose sand. His weight sank slightly into it.

The sand grabbed his feet as he picked his way along the beach.

The waters of Shichirigahama stretched out before him.

Not much wind today. The waves were gently lapping. Not great surfing weather, but perfect for staring out at the ocean.

The light of the setting sun turned the water red, like a portal to another world.

The distant horizon seemed like the edge of that world.

But as far off as it seemed, the horizon was only three miles out. The marathon Minegahara High students ran covered more ground.

It was a weekday, so the beach was largely empty. There was a group of college girls snapping photos with their phones, and a man walking a dog. And one girl in a Minegahara uniform.

She was standing by the water's edge, the wind ruffling her hair.

Sakuta stopped next to her.

"Thanks for waiting, Mai."

"That girl?" she asked softly, looking over at him.

"Walked her to the station."

"'Kay."

A wave rolled in and out.

"Sorry," Mai said.

"Mm?"

"She found you through the photos of us, right?"

Mai was smart enough to guess as much the second Kotomi called out to her and asked about Sakuta.

"I'd rather have a reward than an apology."

"We're not getting intimate."

"Aww."

"I said that was off-limits till you got back on my good side."

Mai was clearly drawing a line in the sand here.

"Then I'll give up on that. But I do have a favor to ask."

Sakuta crouched low, grabbing a pebble out of the sand.

"I'm listening," she said, already skeptical. He hadn't even asked yet. Maybe she thought this was gonna be something weird. How hurtful.

"Do you have time after dinner?"

"Sure. Why?"

"I'd like your help studying."

"Because midterms are next week?"

She looked bored already. Like he'd let her down.

"Sure, that's one reason."

"And what's the other?"

"I want to go to the same college as you."

He spoke facing the ocean, not changing his tone at all.

Mai looked surprised, like she hadn't seen that coming at all. But her expression soon shifted into a smile.

"Who gave you that bright idea?"

"I did a little research. Went to Kunimi for tips on how to make up with your girlfriend."

"I see."

He'd have preferred to pick an easier option. But Mai never

mentioned places she wanted to go or things she wanted to do—but she *had* said she wanted to go to college with him.

He'd run through every memory he had and settled on this.

"I almost forgave you, but not quite."

"Aw, why? Because Kunimi helped?"

"Because you're reluctant."

"Well, I never did like studying."

"But you want to go to college with me."

"Those are two different things."

"You *would* think that."

"If you could teach me in the bunny-girl outfit…"

"Don't push your luck."

She bonked him on the head.

"Ow."

It didn't actually hurt, but he rubbed it anyway, peering up at her.

"Oh, right," she said. Her eyes met his, as if a great idea had just struck her. She looked positively delighted, like she'd found the perfect strategy to drive him up the wall. "I'm thinking about taking a year off first."

"Huh?"

"Well, you said you really wanted to go to college *together*."

This was an even bigger deal than he'd expected.

"Er, wait, but that means…"

"We could spend more time together that way."

"True, but still…"

"You don't like the idea?"

Mai put her hand on her hip. A transparently phony performance. Acting grumpy in a way that made it obvious she was just acting.

"It's not that I don't like it. I'm just…a bit worried."

If Mai waited a year for him, that meant he really couldn't fail the exam. Passing was his only option. And Mai was well aware of that, which was why she looked so delighted. She had cut off any hope of escape with a grin.

"No need to be worried."

"Does that mean you won't be mad if I fail the exam?"

"It means I'll be your home tutor during the year I'm waiting."

"Your efforts may be in vain."

"Sakuta. You love me, right?"

"Well, of course…"

And like that, he had no way out.

"But are you serious about this?"

"It's a good idea, isn't it?"

Her smile was blinding. It sent a powerful message that he needed to quit hemming and hawing. But considering the risk involved, he couldn't quite let it go.

"I just don't want to waste a precious year of your life."

"Time spent with you will hardly be wasted."

The ball he'd tossed out as a test had gone rocketing all the way to the stands in the back.

His only goal had been to get back on her good side, but the price he was paying was far too steep. He may have gotten himself mixed up in something really dangerous. And it was far too late to back out now.

"Anyway, I'd better get home," Mai said, shouldering her bag.

Sakuta stood back up. "Same here."

"Mm?" Mai stopped, surprised. "You're not waiting for Shouko?"

"Sun's already setting, and…no proof she'll even come."

The sun had disappeared behind Enoshima. Not much longer till it was fully dark.

"And Kaede'll be getting hungry."

"I'm good if you're good," Mai said.

"Oh, but I guess I oughta tell her the important thing."

"How?"

Instead of answering, Sakuta started drawing lines in the sand with his shoe. One, then another, then another.

Straight lines and curves. Lines that crossed or joined together.

Mai stood and watched. It took about five minutes.

"Right! Let's go, Mai."

They headed out. He turned back at the top of the stairs, looking down at what he'd written.

A message to Shouko.

When they'd first met, he'd been at rock bottom, running away from everything.

But meeting Shouko had given him the strength to get back up. Her words had kept him going.

He was in high school now. He wasn't exactly sure he was doing the best job of it, but he was living his life. The message he'd left told Shouko what mattered most now.

I've got a girlfriend. From Sakuta.

Mai stood at his side, shaking her head—but looking secretly pleased.

"Should I have added the word *cute*?"

"I think you should keep that part to yourself, Sakuta."

"Well, inside, I'm thinking *really cute*."

"Yeah, yeah."

He meant every word, but it just rolled off her. Still…she took his hand as they started walking, so everything else ceased to matter.

3

They stopped at the grocery store near Fujisawa Station on the way home, and by the time they left, it was dark out. With no trace of the sunset left, the stars were free to stretch out above.

It was just past six. The days were definitely getting shorter. Proof they were well into fall, with winter fast approaching. When the sun set, the temperature dropped, and the wind took on a colder edge.

Sakuta and Mai found their footsteps growing faster.

"Mai," Sakuta said as they left the station crowds behind.

"Mm?" She glanced his way.

"Have you ever thought, 'I don't wanna go to school'?"

"Where'd that come from? Wait, no, I get it," Mai said, answering her own question. "Is this about Kaede?"

"Just…a lot of things today made me think of the past."

Meeting Kotomi Kano for the first time in years. The letter from Shouko. Both things he'd put behind him, and both involved Kaede.

"Oh, but I was thinking about you most of all."

"Spare me."

It was true, but facts did not move her.

"As for school…well, in grade school or junior high, I certainly never wanted to go."

"Really?"

"I mentioned this before, right? Since I was a child star, I didn't fit in and couldn't make friends."

"Oh, right."

"So when I did show up, I'd just have girls talking about me behind my back or stupid boys hitting on me. It sucked. I absolutely hated dealing with it. Everything was so much easier when work kept me out of school."

"I feel like your circumstances are too specific to be helpful for the rest of us."

"You're the one who asked."

She hit him with an extra-powerful glare. These were the same eyes that drew the attention of every audience member whenever she appeared on-screen. Best not to meet this glare head-on. It might freeze him solid.

"I mean, come on…"

"What about you, then?"

"Me?"

"Last year, the hospitalization rumors went around, and you found yourself ostracized. What did you do?"

"You saw for yourself. I just kept going to school like nothing happened. Still show up basically every day."

"How very you."

"Better than twitching at every funny look I get and convincing people I care what they think."

"They probably think you don't care enough." She seemed worn-out for some reason. "It's quite normal to care about how others see you."

"You're on TV, and you still say that?"

"I don't see the connection."

She did, but she segued into the topic anyway. This was a trap. She was trying to make him say it so she could yell at him for it.

"I meant what I said," he replied, being deliberately evasive.

"Rude," Mai hissed, pouting.

But she quickly moved on.

"Schools are unique," she said absently.

"Yeah?"

"It's an obvious thing, but…everyone in class is your age."

"Well, yeah. Kinda the point."

What was she getting at?

"And that makes class the place where it's hardest to ignore the differences between us, the advantages and shortcomings each of us has."

"Oh, I see what you mean."

This was a very Mai way of thinking. Few people would ever reach that conclusion.

Most never thought to examine the nature of schools.

It was too "normal" for people to stop and consider what made them so different.

Kids are thrown into preschool and kindergarten before they're old enough to think like that, and they advance steadily up the ladder to elementary school, junior high, and high school. Everywhere they go, they're surrounded by people their own age.

It's only natural everyone assumes (or convinces themselves) that this is simply how the world works.

And within those same-age groups, everyone is searching for themselves, desperately trying to carve out a place to belong.

But Mai's take was also right. Because everyone is the same age, it forces them to acknowledge even the slightest discrepancies. "He's really tall." "She's cute." "These kids are smarter; those make you laugh"...everyone using one another as measuring sticks. Being around kids their own age allows everyone to explore what makes them different, better, or worse, all so they can apply that knowledge when they're around people outside their age group.

Comparing and contrasting is how kids find themselves.

But just as this system leaves some kids feeling superior, it stifles others.

That was what Mai meant when she called it unique. There were too many mirrors reflecting your sense of self-worth. If you cared about how you looked in each and every one of them, you'd never get anywhere.

"In my case, I was flung into the business so early, I was always around people of all ages, filming movies or TV shows. I always wondered why school had so many children."

"And thinking that's why you can't fit in."

"Like you do any better."

She twisted his cheek. It didn't hurt. This was a very mild pinch.

"But I definitely get why you would struggle," he said.

"Oh?" She scowled at him.

"Well, you're the only one working. You've got a clear difference nobody else can imitate. That's hardly fair."

Working with grown-up actors, directors, and all kinds of other people gave Mai a greater variety of mirrors to see herself in. She'd notice things she could never have learned at school.

Sakuta had gone through a similar experience when he first started working at the restaurant. He'd recently started high school and was feeling all grown up, but just spending time with college students a few years older than him was enough to make him realize how premature that thought was. Those three or four years totally changed how people lived, how they used money, or how far from home they ventured.

There are so many things you can't learn at school. But spending time at school makes you think the whole world works the same way. Schools don't teach you there's a world beyond the classroom.

"I'll concede that point, Sakuta."

"Right?"

"Don't act like you've won."

They fell silent for a moment. As they reached the end of a crosswalk, Mai spoke up again.

"Kaede's changing a little, right?"

"She's getting taller."

Might even be taller than Mai one day.

"That's not what I meant."

"I know."

She was getting pretty comfortable with Mai. At first, Kaede had hid behind the door frame every time Mai came over, but now they were chatting normally.

And recently she'd been putting her junior high school uniform on.

That was not a small change. It was actually quite a big deal.

As they talked about that, they reached their apartment buildings.

"I'll just go change," Mai said and handed him the smaller shopping bag. He'd been carrying the bigger, heavier one from the get-go. It was all the food they'd bought on the way.

"Later." Mai waved and went into her own building.

Sakuta turned the other way and went through the auto-lock doors. They lived across the street from each other.

He took the elevator to the fifth floor.

After getting his key in the lock, he opened the apartment door.

"I'm home!" he announced and put his bags down in the entrance.

Footsteps came pattering toward him.

"Welcome back!" Kaede called, super cheery. She was wearing her panda pajamas again. She had a notebook clutched to her chest—she must have been studying.

Sakuta got his shoes off and took the food to the kitchen.

Kaede followed after. Their cat, Nasuno, came to play underfoot.

"Oh, right, Kaede…"

"What is it?"

"Food'll take a bit."

"Am I going to starve?!"

"Mai's coming over to cook for us."

"Mai's cooking is real tasty, so I can wait!"

Kaede was getting good at cost-benefit analysis.

"I'm gonna go change," Sakuta said.

He went to his room and took off his uniform jacket. Then his pants and shirt. Just as he was down to his boxers, Kaede called out to him.

"What?" he asked, looking over his shoulder.

Kaede was standing in the doorway. He thought she looked a little tense.

"I have an important announcement."

She was still clutching that notebook to her chest, her arms squeezing it tight. Looking closer, he realized it wasn't actually a study notebook. It was the one she used as a diary. It was quite thick and had *Kaede Azusagawa* written on the cover. Sakuta had bought it for her.

"Does it have to be *now*?"

Should he really be hearing this in his underwear?

"Please listen before I lose the courage to say it," she said.

That left him with no choice.

"Very well," he said, turning to face her, boxers and all. "What's the announcement?"

"This!" Kaede opened the notebook and held it up in front of him. "Ta-daaaa!" she sang, a little too late.

The letters were too small to read, so he took a few steps closer.

At the very top, it said:

Kaede's Goals for This Year!

It was written in cute, rounded handwriting.

"What's this?"

"My goals for this year."

"That's definitely what it says."

But it was already mid-October. It was a surprising time to start setting goals for the current year.

He elected not to point this out. Once he started reading the items under the header, such minor details ceased to matter.

Go outside with Sakuta.

Take a walk with Sakuta.

Frolic on the beach with Sakuta.

Having only two and a half months left in the year was nothing compared with these goals.

"Frolic?"

"Frolic!"

"We have to frolic?"

"Yes!"

The list went on.

Ride a train with Sakuta.

Buy pudding with Sakuta.

Go on a date with Sakuta!

The page was completely covered in these.

"Uh, Kaede…"

"What?"

"Are there any goals that don't involve me?"

"There are!"

That was surprising. He'd thought it was a futile question.

"Right here!" Kaede pointed at an item in the middle of the list.

Answer a phone call not from Sakuta.

That certainly qualified.

"……"

It came as kind of a shock.

But it *was* an actual problem that she couldn't answer the phone unless she knew for sure it was him, so it was a good goal to have.

Sakuta's eyes moved down the list of Kaede's goals and finally reached the very bottom. Which said:

Go to school.

This was in slightly smaller letters than the others.

"Well?" Kaede asked.

"It certainly is a *lot* of goals."

"I am committed to results and have processed my thoughts accordingly."

She puffed out her chest proudly. There was not much to puff out. Where was her confidence coming from?

"Oh," he said.

"Yes!"

"You're committing to these results in two and a half months?"

Kaede checked the notebook again.

A frown crept over her face.

"Going outside might be tough…," she said.

She was stuck on the first hurdle. Not surprising. She was a dedicated homebody. She hadn't gone outside in two years. Changing that wouldn't be easy.

"Wh-what do I do?"

"Well, what about adding goals that make you *want* to go outside?"

Setting lofty targets like contact with strangers or going to school were way tougher than achieving ones based purely on her own desires.

"Like what?"

"Hmm…"

Her eyes were filled with anticipation. The answer was right in front of him. There was a panda face on her pajama hood, and its eyes met Sakuta's.

"Go see pandas?"

"Pandas!" Kaede's face lit up. "Giant ones?"

"We can go see the lesser ones, too."

"I'd like to see the pandas!"

Kaede quickly added a new entry to her list.

When she was done, she proudly showed it to him.

Go see pandas with Sakuta.

Sakuta was clearly part and parcel of all these tasks.

"I think I might be able to go outside now!"

"Glad to hear it. Don't force yourself. We can work on your list over time."

"Okay!"

She sounded happy. Thinking positive. A moment later, her stomach growled.

"You need to eat before you commit to these results!"

"When will Mai get here?"

Sakuta had been home for twenty or thirty minutes by this point.

"She is kinda late now, huh?"

No sooner had he said those words than the intercom rang.

Answering the door in his underwear would earn Mai's ire, so he quickly finished changing before she got there.

"Wow," he said as he opened the door. Surprise and delight.

It was Mai outside, of course. But she was wearing an outfit he hadn't seen before.

"That's really cute," he said.

She was wearing a loose-knit sweater that came down to her thighs. All he could see below it were black tights and ankle boots. She'd kept her hair loose to match the sweater, parted to the sides with no braiding. Like junior high school girls of yore, but somehow Mai made it look current and fashionable.

"Thanks."

She accepted his response with aplomb. Like it would take more than this reaction to please her. But she'd have been mad if he didn't react, and madder still if he pointed that out, so he didn't.

"Anyway, come on in," he said.

"Don't ignore me!" another voice said.

There was a smaller blond girl standing next to Mai and sulking.

"Oh, sorry, didn't see you there."

He was lying. He'd spotted her shimmering hair the instant he opened the door.

"But why *are* you here, Toyohama?"

Mai had said her sister had idol lessons today and would be back late. That was the whole reason Mai had picked today to come over and cook.

"Playing hooky?"

"As if!"

"The floor of the dance studio has a hole in it, and they're repairing it today," Mai explained as she took her shoes off. She stepped up into the apartment.

"That place is a real dump." Nodoka made a face.

At this point, footsteps came pattering toward the door.

"Mai, you came! Oh, Nodoka, too!"

Kaede had belatedly come out to greet them. Once, she would've hidden behind the door in the back no matter who it was, watching from a safe distance, so this was significant progress.

"Thanks for having us, Kaede."

"Sure! Mai, you look amazing!"

Kaede appeared to be equally impressed with Mai's look.

The two of them chatted as they headed toward the living room.

"What did you do to my sister, Sakuta?" Nodoka asked while pulling off her long boots. She seemed absolutely sure Sakuta was guilty of something.

"Where'd that come from?"

"I mean…" Nodoka glanced after Mai. "She doesn't usually take that long to pick an outfit."

Sakuta stared at Mai's back, too.

"It's a great outfit," he said. "Filled with possibility."

The sweater came down to her thighs, hiding everything above. Allowing him to imagine what might lie underneath.

"Just to be clear, you may not be able to see them, but she *is* wearing shorts," Nodoka snapped, like she was fending off a pervert.

"Don't destroy my dreams."

Until the box was opened, there was no way to know what lay within. It was very quantum.

Nodoka ignored his protests. "She stood in front of the mirror for ages trying out different hairstyles."

"Huh."

He wondered what she'd tried before settling on this look. He wanted to see them all. He'd have to ask later.

"And if she's going to that much effort…it's for your benefit."

He wasn't sure why Nodoka was so annoyed by this.

"Your outfit is kinda cute, too, Toyohama."

"! K-kinda cute? That's it?"

She turned red like he'd struck a match inside her.

"Okay, then just 'cute.'"

He did think it was cute. She had a pleated checkered skirt with a high waist that emphasized her slim figure. Her blouse had folds in it, too—a nice balance of "cute" and "flashy."

"I-I'm an idol, so I always put in effort in my appearance. I'm not even trying that hard!"

"Mm-hmm, sure."

"……"

He'd agreed with her, but she didn't seem satisfied.

"Nodoka, stop goofing off and come help!"

"I'm not goofing off!"

She pushed past Sakuta and went running down the hall after Mai.

Left behind, Sakuta locked the door and then cheerily headed into the kitchen to savor the sight of Mai in an apron.

4

Mai made a beautiful dish of amberjack and daikon. The fish was perfectly cooked and hearty, and the daikon was impeccably seasoned, not too firm, and not too crisp.

"This amberjack is jacked!" Kaede yelped, giving it her seal of approval. She was stuffing her face. "You're such a good cook, Mai!"

"You can cook like me with a little practice, Kaede."

"I can?!"

"Sure."

"But when Sakuta tried to make amberjack and daikon, it was just jacked up."

"It was," he admitted. He'd most likely overcooked it in an attempt to let the flavors develop. Sadly, the fish had ended up all dried out and nasty. Stewing fish was hard.

Once they'd enjoyed the delicious dinner, Sakuta and Mai cleared the table. He washed the dishes, and she dried them and put them back on the shelf.

Sakuta had tried to do it all himself, but she said, "It'll be faster with two, and you need to study."

No pressure there. She was clearly determined to get this over with so he could spend even more time studying, and he had no right to refuse.

"For midterms?" Nodoka asked. She was in front of the TV, stroking Nasuno.

"Yes, but Sakuta said he wanted to go to the same college as me, so I'm going to start tutoring him."

"Huh? You're going to college?" Nodoka asked.

Apparently, this was news to her. She yelped so loud Nasuno jumped up and ran off.

It *was* sort of shocking, really.

Mai was a famous, successful actress. *The* Mai Sakurajima. With her talent and fame, lots of people would assume she'd focus on her career after graduating high school. And Mai's work situation made going to college a real challenge. Nodoka was deep enough in the business to know exactly how tough it would be.

"I'd like to. If Sakuta can pass, that is."

He was clearly a fundamental part of her plans now.

"But where?"

"A public school in Yokohama somewhere."

"Maybe I should try for the same place."

"Don't you dare, Toyohama."

"Huh? Why not?"

"That would be one less passing slot."

Nodoka's blond hair made her seem a little like the frivolous type, but she actually had solid grades. She was currently attending a demanding girls' school in Yokohama.

"If that's what you're worried about, you're doomed already."

"Even if I have the lowest passing score, a pass is a pass," Sakuta said. "But are you actually planning on going to college, Toyohama? I thought you were gonna become a top idol and make me eat my words."

"There's a lot of competition in the idol biz."

"So?"

"So I'm gonna go to college and be an educated idol."

That played against her dye job and "gal" makeup, but it might actually work in her favor.

"Then you might as well try to aim for the best school in Japan."

"I guess you have a point, but…"

Nodoka's eyes began to wander, like she was hunting for an excuse.

"In other words, you just want to go to the same school as your sister, huh? Your motives are *so* suspect."

"You're one to talk! Like you're going to college to prepare for the future!"

"I'm preparing for my future with Mai."

Nodoka's jaw dropped. She gave Sakuta a look like even speaking to him was a waste of time.

"What do you think life *is*, Sakuta?"

"A way of killing time until you die."

"…You're a clown. An absolute clown."

"Maybe this is hard for an aspiring idol like you to understand, Toyohama, but life isn't just about where you end up."

She had to think about that one. Ultimately, she didn't really seem to get what he was saying.

"So what qualifies as a life by your definition?" she asked.

"Mm, well…," he began—but then the phone rang.

The landline.

"Who could that be?"

There was an eleven-digit number on the display. Someone's cell phone. It looked familiar—and then his heart skipped a beat.

That was Shouko's number. The younger one.

"Hello," he answered, feigning calm.

"Er, um, this is Makinohara. Good evening."

The voice that came through sounded quite young. Clearly, this really was the junior high school Shouko. And she called herself Makinohara, not "Shouko" like the letter had.

"Good evening to you, too."

"I'm sorry it took me so long to return your phone call."

"Oh, you mean yesterday? That's okay. I said I'd call back but never did, huh? Sorry."

"So, uh, what was it about?"

"I was just checking on something."

His eyes met Mai's. He was pretty sure she'd worked out it was Shouko by now.

"Checking what?"

"Did you leave a letter in our mailbox?"

"No."

She sounded baffled. He could picture her tilting her head to one side and blinking at him.

"Cool, that's all."

"Sorry I couldn't be more help."

"Nah, thanks for getting back to me."

"Okay."

A grown-up's voice called her name. Probably Shouko's mom.

"S-sorry. I've gotta get back to the exam room."

"You're in the hospital?"

"Y-yes…um…I came in for monitoring a couple of days ago."

It sounded like she regretted letting that slip. Clearly, she hadn't planned to tell him.

"B-but I'm totally fine," she said, talking very fast. "Really, I swear. I'll be checking out tomorrow."

Shouko didn't want him worrying about her, so Sakuta didn't press the point any further.

"Well, bring Hayate over to play again some time. Kaede would like that."

"Okay! Then good night, Sakuta."

"Good night."

She hung up. A moment later, he did, too.

"Shouko?" Mai asked.

"Yep. Like I thought, she didn't know about the letter."

"Oh."

"Letter?" Nodoka seemed confused.

"Er, um," Kaede said, grabbing his arm as he tried to step away.

"Mm? What's up?"

"I-if Shouko calls again, can I be the one to answer?"

"Oh, sure."

"Kaede, you want to answer the phone?" Mai was surprised.

"Yes! It's one of my goals!"

"Goals?"

"These!"

Kaede held up the list she had been working on, showing them to Mai and Nodoka.

"Right here!" she said as she pointed to the phone entry.

"Ah, goals for this year." Mai glanced over at Sakuta like she'd had an idea. "Can I grab a pen?"

He took a ballpoint from the stash by the phone and handed it to her.

Mai put Kaede's notebook down on the table and wrote something in it.

Sakuta leaned in to look. It said:

Visit Mai's place with Sakuta.

"I can come over?!"

"Sure! Come over anytime."

Kaede smiled, looking sheepish.

"What's gotten you so motivated, Kaede?"

"I realized something recently."

"What?" Nodoka asked.

"If I don't learn to be independent, Sakuta will never get married."

That was a shocking revelation.

"Tell me more."

It had never occurred to Sakuta that Kaede was making lists of goals for the sake of his future marriage.

"I mean, whoever you get married to will have to take me, too."

"That's a plus."

"A big one! I mean, no! It's not."

"Mai would happily take you."

He glanced her way, but Mai didn't meet his eye.

"I wouldn't mind if you were there," she said, patting Kaede's head.

Sounded like there were no problems.

"But if you can learn how to be independent, I think that's a good thing. Would you like to practice talking on the phone with me now?"

"With you?"

"Yes. I could call from Sakuta's room, and you could answer."

"O-oh! I want to try."

"You've got it."

Before Kaede's resolve could waver, Mai got up and moved to Sakuta's room. She no longer had any qualms about waltzing in there whenever she pleased.

When she'd been in Nodoka's body, it had functionally been her room. Sakuta felt that from a relationship perspective, the act of entering his bedroom ought to carry a *little* more tension.

The door closed, but the phone didn't ring right away.

This was likely because Mai had powered her phone off. She'd seen Kaede flinch before when it rang or vibrated, and she was likely being considerate of that.

After waiting maybe thirty seconds, the phone rang.

Sakuta, Kaede, and Nodoka all turned to stare at the phone. The number on it was definitely Mai's cell phone.

"……"

Kaede stood frozen to the spot.

"Don't worry. That's Mai for sure."

"I—I know."

She slowly reached for the receiver.

Her hand closed around it, but lifting it was a bit too much.

Her fingers trembled.

She stayed like that until it went to the answering machine.

"Leave your message after the tone."

The machine beeped, and they heard Mai's voice.

"My name is Mai Sakurajima. I'm dating your brother."

Mai was formally introducing herself. Likely in the hopes of reassuring Kaede.

"I'm calling today because I hoped to speak to you, Kaede."

Kaede was still shaking.

Sakuta placed his hands gently on her shoulders.

"It'll be okay."

"R-right."

Kaede took a deep breath, then another. Mai kept talking, not giving up on her.

At last, Kaede screwed her eyes tightly closed and lifted the receiver.

"A-Azusagawa speaking!" she squeaked. Her nerves were obvious.

But she *was* holding the receiver to her ear.

"Well done, Kaede. You did it!" Mai's voice called from down the hall.

"I did it!" Kaede said, turning around to face Sakuta and exploding with happiness.

Her eyes glistened—tears of joy and relief welling up at the edges of them.

"Hello, Kaede? Can you hear me?"

"Y-yes! I can hear you!" Kaede said as she put the phone back to her ear.

"I guess that means you can answer if it's me calling, huh?"

"I—I think so, yes!"

"Then I'll have to call again sometime."

"I'm looking forward to it!"

The whole call only lasted a minute. But this was a huge step for Kaede. Genuinely huge. Sakuta was honestly shocked this day had arrived.

Kaede took a few more deep breaths and then slowly put the phone back on the hook.

"Good for you, Kaede," Sakuta said.

And as he did, it happened. All the strength left her body, like the strings that had been holding her up suddenly snapped.

"Kaede!"

He reached out to catch her and managed to pull her to him. Together, they sat down heavily on the floor.

If he'd been a second later, she'd have hit her head.

"Uh, Kaede?"

"What? What's wrong?" Mai came out of his room. She'd heard the thud and come running.

"I dunno. Kaede just…" Nodoka glanced up at Mai. She'd been crouching next to them, peering at Kaede's face.

"Kaede?"

"I-I'm okay!" Kaede said, forcing a smile. She looked utterly exhausted.

Plus, he could feel her body burning up. He couldn't take her word for it.

He reached up and put a hand on her forehead.

"……"

She was definitely running a fever.

"Sorry," Mai said, crouching down next to her. "Maybe we went a little too fast."

"No! You helped me achieve one of my goals."

Kaede might've been struggling to smile at Mai, but she was clearly proud of herself, too. She'd already managed to reach one of her goals. Like she said, that was undoubtedly a good thing. Sakuta was happy for her. She'd done something she hadn't been able to do for two whole years.

"Mm-hmm. You did great, Kaede," Mai said, rubbing her head.

Kaede giggled like she was ticklish.

"But I think that's enough for today. Nodoka and I will head home. You make sure Kaede rests up, Sakuta."

This was definitely not the time to study. Sakuta nodded in wholehearted agreement.

He tucked Kaede into bed and then briefly stepped out of the apartment to walk Mai and Nodoka to the front entrance.

"It's hard to understand," Mai said on the elevator. Almost to herself.

He didn't have to ask what she meant by that. Sakuta felt the same way.

Both of them could answer the phone easily. Even painfully shy people had no problems answering calls from people they knew.

But that was very hard for Kaede. She had to work like crazy to achieve something that came naturally for most. And even when she did it, the stress of it was so intense that it left her exhausted and feverish. The toll was simply that great.

Like Mai said, it was hard to grasp Kaede's perspective. Perhaps it was even impossible to truly understand without having personally experienced it. Especially when it was something easy.

They reached the ground floor without saying much of anything else.

"See you tomorrow," Mai said once they were outside. Sending him right back to Kaede.

"Lemme know if anything else comes up," Nodoka said, looking worried.

"Will do," Sakuta said, like he wasn't concerned at all.

There was no need for Nodoka to be that upset.

Mai and Nodoka vanished into their building. Sakuta waited until the glass doors slid shut behind them, and then he turned back to his place.

"Coming in, Kaede," he said, knocking on the door.

She tried to sit up.

"You keep resting."

"Where's my notebook?" she asked. Her face flushed slightly from the fever.

"In the living room. I'll grab it for you."

He left her room and found the notebook on the table. He picked it up and headed back in.

"Here."

Kaede took the notebook and drew a red circle next to the entry on answering the phone. She showed it to him, looking proud.

"At this rate, I might go outside tomorrow!"

"Sure."

"And go see pandas!"

"That pandas will be worried if you're still not feeling well.".

"That would be bad! I'd better go right to sleep."

She lay down, and he took the notebook from her.

As he did, he saw a mark on her wrist. At first, he thought it was a trick of the light, but it wasn't.

It was a bruise.

That wasn't a good sign. He felt a shudder run down his spine.

Fighting back his fears, he checked to make sure Kaede was asleep, then rolled her pajama sleeve up.

Splotches of purple covered her arm. All the way up to her elbow. What kind of blow could do that to you?

"……"

It was a painful reminder.

He closed his eyes, seeing it all again. Awful memories that would be with him the rest of his life. And the bruise on her arm had dredged them all back up.

Two years ago, when the bullying had reached its peak, mysterious bruises and cuts had started appearing on Kaede's body every time she saw a post online or a message from one of the bullies.

Kaede's Adolescence Syndrome clearly hadn't gone anywhere. Even after moving far away, even after cutting her off from everything online and limiting her contact with other people—all that had done was temporarily stop the bruises and cuts from appearing. It hadn't solved the core problem.

Kaede's heart still hadn't been saved.

The ugly purple bruise on her frail white arm was proof Kaede had simply been frozen in time for two years. That much was all too obvious.

Maybe it was time for her to overcome it.

Kaede was trying to change. Maybe she had to walk this thorny path to achieve the goals in her notebook.

It would be a long, hard road.

But Sakuta wasn't afraid. He was ready.

He was past being surprised by something like this. There was no need to fear it.

He'd been ready for this day for a long time now.

Chapter
2

kaede Quest

1

He could hear the sound of waves.

They rolled up the sands and then pulled out with a noise like someone gasping aloud.

This was the beach at Shichirigahama.

Sakuta was standing there, surrounded by familiar sights— younger than he was now.

There was no color in this wave-lapped scene. The sky, sea, and horizon were all shades of gray.

Even with a foggy mind, Sakuta knew right away this had to be a dream.

A dream of two years ago, when he'd been in the last year of junior high.

A dream of the time his heart had shattered to pieces.

And a dream of the time he first met Shouko Makinohara.

"Did you know?"

Once again, she was suddenly next to him, talking like she was sharing something deep and meaningful.

He stood quite close, maybe three yards away. He could see Enoshima behind her.

"Shichirigahama is actually one *ri* long. Weird they named it 'seven *ri*,' huh?"

"You always make a habit of interrupting people when they're thinking, Shouko?"

"I make a habit of giving you the advice you need, Sakuta."
She grinned at him.

"……"

"Ah, just now, you thought, 'She's so obnoxious!' didn't you?"

"Absolutely."

"But about two percent of you was thinking how nice it is to have a nice older girl helping you."

She nodded to herself, like it was obvious.

"That's even more obnoxious," he growled, glaring at the ocean.

"There it is! You're so easily embarrassed."

His grumbles had no effect on her. None. She just looked at him like a mother would an angry toddler. Protesting felt like a waste of time.

"Thinking about your sister again?"

And the moment he let his guard down, she spoke softly, cutting right to the heart of the matter. With all the sensitivity she'd seemingly lacked a moment before.

"I was thinking about you, Shouko."

"Oh, so you were thinking about sex. You are one hormonal teen! I'll allow it."

He really wished she'd stop willfully misinterpreting these things. Or accepting them at face value.

"No," he said, a tad forcefully.

"So it *was* about your sister, then."

This was true, but he didn't want to admit it, so instead he said, "I was wondering why you believed me."

He'd been wondering that since they first met.

"Mm?"

"Nobody else would listen at all. Not about Kaede's cuts and bruises, or about Adolescence Syndrome."

The bullying had eaten away at Kaede's heart. Eventually, it turned into full-blown Adolescence Syndrome, and the pain in her heart became cuts and bruises on her body.

You suck.

A post online that made her arm split open like a knife had cut into her.

Die, creep (lol).

A text she got that left a huge bruise on her thigh.

No matter how patiently he explained, nobody believed him. His mother saw it with her own eyes but couldn't accept the truth, distancing herself from Kaede instead. The doctors they saw were convinced it was self-harm and wouldn't hear a word about Adolescence Syndrome. They dismissed Sakuta's claims as the prattling of a child.

The more he explained, the more desperate he got, and the more hostile everyone involved became.

They all thought the same thing.

They all thought he was full of shit. No matter how much he begged for help, all he got in return was contempt.

No matter how loud he yelled "It's true!" nobody heard.

And it created a vicious cycle. Even his closest friends started keeping their distance, one after another.

Before he knew it, he was all alone.

Azusagawa's lost it.

Once someone posted that online, it spread like wildfire, and everyone in class started avoiding him. No one at school, not even the teachers, wanted anything to do with him.

No one tried to find out what was really happening. None of his friends asked what had happened. Everyone would rather believe a lie. Because "everyone" said it was true.

Looking back, he understood. Going along with the crowd and sticking with the general consensus was important. That was what years of school had taught them to do. Even if you were sure you were different or special, you'd been taught the smart play was to hide those feelings and avoid standing out.

So for the majority of students, what others said about Sakuta was truer than anything Sakuta himself had to say. After all, "everyone" said it. Popular opinion carried far more weight than the truth of the matter. For classmates who didn't know Sakuta well, that was all there was to it. Plain and simple.

But the result was that "everyone" had a negative perception of him, and he found himself facing what felt like a monster.

No amount of struggling would lead him to victory. It had no tangible form, so he had no way of harming it. It didn't take long for him to realize fighting was futile.

And when he realized that, something inside him snapped. He could feel it happen.

He was right, he knew he was right, but they'd made him "wrong." The world was just not fair. It was so stupid and messed up, he just started laughing. A hollow, empty laugh.

And all the color drained from his world.

The world became a gray place.

"There are as many worlds as there are people," Shouko said, staring at the horizon. "Just as the horizon I'm looking at is closer than the one you see."

She crouched a bit so she was looking up at his face from below.

Like she was emphasizing that his height advantage let him see farther than she could.

"And this sea breeze!" she said, straightening up and throwing her arms out.

As if trying to hug the wind. Her hair streamed out behind her.

"Some people will think it feels good, and others will hate it for making their skin and hair all sticky."

Shouko was clearly the former. She closed her eyes, seeming to enjoy the sensation.

"My point is…"

"Everyone has a different idea of justice? I know that."

He was being a bit curt, but Shouko just laughed.

"As if I'd say something that sounds like it came right out of the mouth of a teenage boy. Doesn't just saying the word *justice* feel embarrassing?"

"Then what *did* you mean?"

"You're agonizing over a monster you can't defeat. But I say that means you have potential."

"Patronizing."

"I *am* older than you. I have a right to be."

She shot him a triumphant look as she puffed out her chest.

"......"

"Ah! You just thought 'You're older? With tits that small?' right?"

"No. And I dunno about 'agonizing,' either. I just know life is devoid of dreams or hope, and I'm feeling shitty about it. Leave me alone."

"Never!" she said. But her tone was soft, so it didn't feel aggressive.

"Huh?"

"I'm not gonna leave you alone."

Her eyes caught his. She was serious, but there was also a trace of a smile. An expression of great kindness.

It left him speechless.

"We met like this for a reason. You may have no dreams or hope, but I've lived a little longer than you have, and I've got some gorgeous advice to offer."

She was sounding increasingly theatrical.

"Whoever heard of gorgeous advice?"

Shouko ignored that, turning back to the ocean.

The look on her face was so beautiful that he found himself looking out to sea as well. A horizon slightly farther than the one she saw. Was there something out there?

"My life hasn't had a lot of dreams or hope in it, either," she said.

What did that mean? He couldn't bring himself to ask. Shouko had turned back to him, and their eyes met—and she shook her head.

"But I have found meaning in my life."

"……"

"You see, Sakuta. I think living makes us kinder."

"…And that's the point?"

"I've lived this long so that I could become as kind as I am now."

"……"

"Each day, I try to be just a little nicer than I was the day before."

"……"

He didn't know why.

He didn't know, but her words sank deep inside him, warming him from within. The feeling enveloped him like a blanket warmed in the light of the sun.

Sakuta felt a burning heat well up at the back of his nose. Gushing upward with considerable force. He had no way of stopping it. The tear levees burst immediately, and drops started spilling from his eyes.

They fell like rain on the sand at his feet, like a warm shower of tears.

A ray of light appeared in his gray world. Sakuta looked up, drawn to it. Color was returning to his world, centered around Shouko. The deep blue of the sea, the pale blue of the sky—all the colors were coming back.

He gritted his teeth, not even trying to wipe his tears. "Shouko," he said.

"What?" she said with a smile.

"I hope I can live like you do."

She looked pleased. "You can." She accepted his feelings, grinning ear to ear. "You know how not being understood makes you suffer, Sakuta. That will make you nicer than anyone. You'll find someone to help in no time."

His tears left his vision blurry. He couldn't quite make out the look on her face. But it was Shouko, so he was sure her smile was as bright as the sun above. He never doubted that.

That was the last time they ever spoke.

When he woke up, his eyelashes were stuck together.

He'd been crying in his sleep.

He tried to reach up and rub the dried tears away, but his arm wouldn't budge.

It was too heavy—no, there was a weight on it. Someone was lying on top of him.

He looked down.

As suspected, his sister was resting there, sleeping peacefully.

"Yo, Kaede," he called.

No response.

Just the sound of her breathing.

"Yo!" he said again.

"Your amberjack is jacked up," she said. Awfully specific for talking in her sleep. He would have to ask Mai for a few tips so he could make that dish better.

"C'mon, Kaede. Wake up."

"…Jacked?"

"You're still saying that?"

He wasn't getting anywhere.

He forcibly yanked his arm out from under her and shook Kaede's shoulder.

"Mm? Hmm…"

As she grumbled, her eyes fluttered open.

"Morning, Kaede."

"Good morning," she said and yawned.

"Get up, would you? You're heavy."

"I am?! But I'm your little sister!"

"That has nothing to do with your weight."

"But I'm aiming to be the kind of sister you treat like an emotional support puppy!"

"Suit yourself, but size-wise, you've already failed."

Kaede was certainly growing up. The latest data available had her another half inch taller, and she was now a little over five foot four. Not exactly cute puppy sized. More like cute large dog sized.

"What a shocking discovery…"

"Also, that goal wasn't in your notebook."

"That's because it is the little sister ideal I was secretly gunning for."

"I see. Shame."

"Yes, it really is. I'll have to use this failure as a springboard to step up my practice for going outside."

A humble, optimistic statement like a young athlete interviewed after a loss. He wanted to throw his support behind her, but first he had to assess her physical condition.

He put a hand on her forehead.

"……"

It was still hot. She'd been lying on him a moment before, so he'd already had his suspicions. It would probably be better to leave going outside for a later day.

"When your fever subsides and you're in better health," he said.

"Okay. A famous person on TV said if you have health, you can do anything!"

"Famous people say good things sometimes."

"I thought so!"

"But for today, get some rest."

"Okay! I'll try real hard to rest so I can try real hard tomorrow!"

2

She'd said *tomorrow*, but the next day—Wednesday—Kaede's temperature was still running high.

The thermometer showed 99 degrees.

A mild fever, though one that would still leave you feeling pretty worn out.

She had no other noticeable symptoms, so she probably wasn't sick, but her fever failed to subside when he checked Thursday morning, and again on Friday morning.

This was frustrating. Since it was likely caused by psychological instability, taking fever reducers wasn't going to help much. They did seem to temporarily drop her temperature, but the moment the medicine wore off, she went right back to hovering around the 99-degree mark.

Each time he checked the readout on the digital thermometer, Kaede looked frustrated. She felt slightly tired but had no problems moving around, and being forced to stay in bed was boring her silly.

Trying to respect her positivity, Sakuta suggested, "Maybe think up some strategies to use once your fever goes down."

"Strategies?"

"Or even just rehearse it in your mind."

"That sounds cool! Like a professional operating on a global scale!"

"The top players all do it before any big match."

"I want to be a top player!"

"Then you'll have to imagine yourself going outside."

"First, I open the door!"

"With no shoes?"

"First, I put shoes on!"

"Maybe you should change clothes, too."

Kaede usually wore her panda pajamas around the house.

"First, I want to change into the cutest outfit I have."

"Fashion is vital."

"Very."

"That's the spirit. Visualize yourself winning this battle, Kaede."

"I will!"

They had a lot of conversations like this.

After talking to her like he usually did, Kaede seemed to be in high spirits. He detected no signs of any anxiety. Which meant he had no clue how to help.

The fever was caused by something inside her that Sakuta couldn't see.

All he could do was cheer her on.

But telling her to try harder would just put pressure on her, and he didn't think this was a problem that willpower could solve.

Perhaps other grown-ups would look at her situation and say she wasn't putting in enough effort. A lot of old-fashioned teachers had said as much when she was getting bullied. As if a Showa-era talk of gumption would be able to help a Heisei-born junior high school girl.

The question remained—what should he do?

With no effective medicine, all he could do was wait patiently.

Friday, October 17, after school, Sakuta worked his shift at the restaurant with all the enthusiasm his wages deserved. He finished ringing up a couple of male students and muttered "Now what?" under his breath.

Voicing his uncertainty this way was a minor thing, but it helped relieved the stress mounting within.

It was after eight, and the number of customers was on the downswing. More and more seats were emptying up.

They were most likely through the worst of the dinner rush.

Sakuta left the register, bussed the empty table, and ferried the dishes into the back.

He put the hamburger steak platter and rice dishes by the sinks.

"More for you," he said.

The college student washing the dishes said, "Got it," and Sakuta returned to the front of house.

As he did, he heard a dramatic sigh.

"I just dunno…"

This was coming from a petite girl.

"That was one huge sigh."

"Whaaa—?! Senpai?!"

Tomoe Koga jumped a whole step backward in surprise. She was his junior both at school and here. A very fashionable, modern schoolgirl, she wore her hair short and woke up at six every morning to get it perfect. It looked great today, too.

"Worried because your butt got bigger again?" he said.

Her hands snapped around behind her. She glared up at him.

"I-it hasn't gotten bigger, and why'd you say *again*?"

"Depressed about the tests next week, then?"

"Well, you're not wrong, but…"

"But what?"

"The culture festival," she muttered, scowling.

"What about it?"

"It's coming up next month!"

"Where?"

"At our school!"

"Huh."

"Have you completely lost it, senpai? It's, like, a critical event in any high schooler's life!"

She seemed as baffled as she was surprised. Like it was unbelievable he didn't care.

"Culture festivals are something a small percentage of in-crowd kids get all worked up about. They hit peak giddy, pair off into couples, and make some precious memories together. Not my scene."

Come to think of it, when second term started, there had been some chatter about what their class would do. He was pretty sure Yuuma's girlfriend, Saki Kamisato, had seized control of the whole shebang. Sakuta mostly slept through homerooms, so he didn't really remember the details.

Plus, he'd spent most of last month dealing with a round of Adolescence Syndrome that had left Mai and Nodoka in each other's bodies, so he definitely hadn't had any bandwidth to care about what his class was doing for the culture festival even if he wanted to.

"You never disappoint, senpai," Tomoe said. This sounded like praise, but her eyes were filled with pity. He took offense to that. "It's impressive, really," she added.

"How so?"

"You're dating Sakurajima, which oughta instantly put you in the winner's circle, but somehow you still can't fit in, as per usual."

"And as per usual, you're worrying yourself silly about what to do for the culture festival or who's gonna take which shift, right?"

"O-our class knows what we're doing! We're still arguing over the other thing, though…"

He'd been talking off the cuff, but it looked like he'd hit the nail on the head. Tomoe shot him a baleful glare, puffing her cheeks out. She must have thought he was making fun of her. That probably wasn't inaccurate.

"So what is your class doing?"

"A haunted house."

"Pfft, with a face that cute?"

"God, you're obnoxious sometimes. My face doesn't have anything to do with it! A-and I'm not cute!"

"I think it's highly relevant. You dressed as a ghost would *never* be scary."

If she tried dressing up as a *nekomata*, she'd just look like she was doing some cute cat-girl cosplay.

"Th-then show up on the day! I promise I'll get a scream out of you."

"Nah, I'm good. Never been into classic horror. That stuff just doesn't scare me. I mean, look, there's a long-haired girl ghost behind you right now."

He pointed over Tomoe's shoulder, then smiled, bobbed his head, and waved.

"E-eep!" Tomoe shrieked and leaped a foot in the air.

"I'm kidding, but…mm?"

He must have spooked her good, because Tomoe had fallen on her backside next to the register. And she'd screamed loud enough that all the customers had turned to stare.

"S-sorry," she said, scrambling back to her feet. She gave Sakuta an accusative, teary-eyed glare.

"Are you even capable of working in a haunted house?"

"A mite too late ta go askin' that!" she howled.

"Uhhh, right. I guess so."

She was so rattled, she'd lapsed back into her native dialect, and he barely understood a word she said.

"I can see why that would have you all depressed."

"It's not the ghosts that are bothering me. You said it yourself."

"Mm? What did I say?"

"We're taking turns being the ghosts, but figuring out the shift schedule's got everyone on edge."

Such a typical source of conflict.

"You can't just split it up so everyone's working with their usual crowd?"

The number might vary a bit, but that method would make everything straightforward.

"Yeah, but once you start pairing groups of girls and guys up, it all goes to hell."

"Seems like the popular folks should just stick together to settle things quickly. Like I said."

Classroom groups tended to naturally form without anyone actively saying or doing anything. The organic hierarchy was strangely compelling, and neither the top- nor bottom-tier students could ignore it. Try to go against the flow, and people would be all, "What's your problem?" and then you'd be outcast.

In Sakuta's view, people who said "What's your problem?" were the ones with the problem, which was why they looked down on anyone not like them.

Exactly when had Japan reverted to feudalism anyway? Sakuta was a citizen of this country and felt he ought to have been informed.

"If it was that easy, I wouldn't be griping. But somehow we ended up drawing lots…"

Tomoe looked very shifty suddenly. That seemed like a clear sign of guilt. Sakuta instantly knew who'd proposed this plan…

"So your group ended up paired with the hot guys?"

"Urp…"

"And now the hot girls are mad at you?"

Tomoe gave up and admitted it. "…Y-yeah."

"You always have the most typical high school girl problems, Koga."

"That's because I *am* a high school girl."

In Tomoe's case, things were made even more complicated because she had originally been part of the popular girls group. She'd left after a quarrel. Following a brief period of isolation, she'd wound up with her current group of friends. So this was all really unfortunate.

"If only the guys were complaining, too, but no, they're all cool with it."

"Meaning they're all, 'Koga's pretty cute, so whatever,' I take it?"

"……"

Tomoe turned red. Half mortified, half mad. It seemed she was well aware of this. She always did know how to read a room. Maybe the dumb dudes had been a bit too happy when the lots were drawn. And oblivious to how scary girl group dynamics could be.

"I'm impressed, Koga."

"Nothing impressive about this."

"You've evolved into a being of pure evil."

She *was* the petite devil. Totally living up to that nickname.

"This is a real problem! You're such a jerk. Horribad."

Tomoe turned her back on him, sulking.

This left her looking at a booth across the hall. A group of four junior high school boys occupied it. They were all staring at their phones or portable gaming consoles, chattering as they played. There was a burst of laughter. They were talking about an RPG they were into.

Levels, weapon upgrades, how unfair the last boss was…sounded like fun.

"Argh, I wish life was as easy as games," Tomoe said.

"You play games, Koga?"

She didn't seem the type. Or maybe she was the type who was hopelessly bad at them.

"Just on my phone. Nana likes 'em, so I keep her company."

"Huh."

"Senpai, that's your 'Stop being so desperate to fit in, you don't even like it' face."

"I was wondering if you were actively trying to get guys to like you more."

"Huh? Playing games does that?"

"Yeah, gives them an excuse to start a conversation with you."

"……"

This notion silenced Tomoe. Something like that must have actually happened.

"But I get what you're saying."

The booth boys were still talking excitedly.

"Fighting monsters gets you XP. You level up, learn some skills, get better spells, try again if you die, and beat the Demon Lord to a pulp at the end, and bam, you're the hero who saved the world."

"I'm not being *that* cynical," Tomoe said.

He ignored her. "But life isn't that easy."

Tomoe's opponent was the classroom mood. Kaede's was her own anxieties. Neither Demon Lord was visible to the naked eye.

They didn't have the ultimate weapons or spells at their disposal. And a good old-fashioned beatdown wouldn't solve their problems.

And worst of all, these Demon Lords were created by other people. An unconscious by-product of mob mentality.

He was pretty sure he'd played games where people's fears gave the Demon Lord power, and that felt accurate to the real world. Demon Lords were created and sustained by human minds.

"……"

"Something on your mind, senpai?" Tomoe asked.

It wasn't really a question. She'd gleaned the truth from his silence.

"Nah…I was just wondering, when's the culture festival again?"

"You're such a bad liar."

She apparently wasn't buying that one. But she didn't try to force the truth out of him, either. Respecting his feelings on the matter.

"It's November 3. Culture Day," she said, dutifully answering his fake question. Such a good kohai. Guys liked her for a reason.

"You know what time you'll be haunting yet?"

"Nope."

She gave him a look, as if wondering why he was asking.

"Lemme know when you settle the shifts."

"You're gonna come?" She seemed skeptical.

"You want to try to make me scream, right?"

"Oh, that's definitely gonna happen."

She flashed him a cheeky grin. And as she did, the bell on the door rang. New customers. Tomoe went to seat them. "Welcome!" she called. No trace of her earlier gloom remained.

Pleased with that, Sakuta went back to work himself.

Sakuta worked the rest of his shift and punched out exactly on time at nine. His card emerged from the machine with *21:00* stamped on it.

"And we're outta here."

He quickly changed out of his server uniform and headed back home to Kaede.

The restaurant was located right outside Fujisawa Station, and their place was about a ten-minute walk away.

When he got to his building, he checked the mailbox before hopping on the elevator. There was a part of him that was still curious if any more letters from "Shouko" might show up.

It was empty again, though. Just a flyer for a pizza joint.

"Welp, if it comes, it comes."

No point waiting for something without a reason to believe it was coming. This wasn't something hopes and desires could solve any more than trying real hard. It was all up to *her*.

Waiting would just wear him down. He had to put it out of his mind until something actually happened.

Telling himself this, Sakuta stepped into the elevator.

He reached his floor and opened the door to his apartment.

"Welcome home!"

And was surprised by Kaede, who'd been lurking beside the front door.

"Uh, sure, I'm back…"

There was no denying that startled him a bit.

Kaede dashed off back inside.

Why is she in such a hurry? Is something going on?

"He really did come home!" he heard her saying.

It sounded like she was talking to somebody. But there weren't any other shoes by the door. And Kaede was way too shy. If someone rang the intercom and Sakuta wasn't home, she would entrust everything to the might of the answering machine. Even when he was home, the most she could manage was to watch him handle it from a distance. There was no way she could actually let someone in on her own.

"You were right, Mai!"

Sakuta shucked his shoes off and stepped into the living room. Kaede was on the phone. She had the receiver cradled in both hands, holding it to her ear.

Naturally, he knew who she was talking to now.

Mai had left school after fourth bell that day. She had to film a variety show that afternoon. They must have wrapped already.

"Okay, I'll let you talk to him.

Kaede held the receiver out to him.

"Mai?"

"Welcome back."

"Glad to be home."

"I was watching you from my balcony, but you didn't look up."

"Oh? Just now?"

"Yep."

"Ahhh, that explains it."

This was why Kaede had been standing at the door.

"How's Kaede doing?"

He glanced toward her. She was—for some reason—happily watching him talk on the phone.

"Smiling a lot." His reply was very literal.

"Good. Glad to hear it." Mai sounded relieved. "I said I had that show to film at the studio, right?"

"Yep."

"It was a medical-themed show, and this episode was all about stress, so after we finished, I asked one of the experts about Kaede."

Sakuta could guess why they'd ask Mai to be on a show like that, given recent events. The coverage of their relationship had been intense. Mai would be able to talk about the stress of the public eye in an immediate, attention-grabbing way.

"He said attempting something new probably startled her mind and body."

"I had a feeling, yeah."

She could answer phones from someone besides Sakuta. That was it, but Kaede had gone way outside her comfort zone to make it happen. Even if she handled the challenge well, it left her heart racing.

This wasn't particular to Kaede. There were all sorts of events and experiences that could leave you a wreck for days. In Kaede's case, things just had a more dramatic effect.

Kaede caught Sakuta glancing her way, but she couldn't hear what Mai was saying. She shot him a puzzled look.

"The body and mind will usually recover in time, but he said in a situation like Kaede's, repetition is really important."

"Oh?"

"A new experience becomes far less novel if you do it over and over again, right? Once it becomes a normal part of life, it won't be reason for alarm anymore. So it's better *not* to do it once and stop."

"So that's why you called?"

"Yes—and I saw you coming home from my balcony. I considered running this by you first, but…I figured it would be a good idea to have her make a second go at it while the memories of a successful attempt are still fresh. She seem okay?"

As far as he could tell, she was having a great time. Sakuta reached for her forehead.

She still had a fever, but she had it all day, so this didn't seem like a major change. Sakuta propped the phone between his ear and shoulder, took Kaede's arm, and rolled up her sleeve. The bruise running from her elbow to her wrist was still there, but it had been gradually fading over the last few days. Now it was almost gone.

"Thermometer," was all he said out loud. Then he mimed pinning one under his arm.

"Got it." She grabbed the thermometer from the table nearby, slipping it inside her pajamas.

"As far as I can tell, she's fine. Better than this morning, even."

"Whew."

Kaede had the thermometer lodged in her pajamas. They waited a moment, and then it beeped. She pulled it out and showed it to Sakuta, like a cat offering up a catch.

The digital display showed 98.8 degrees. Still slightly elevated, but the lowest readout she'd had all week. Since the last phone call had immediately spiked her temperature, this was much more promising.

She'd done it not just once but twice now—each success stacked and eased Kaede's anxiety. Every victory would slowly build the foundation for her newfound courage and confidence.

And the more successful attempts she had, the closer they'd get to Kaede's ultimate goal of going to school. Sakura wanted to believe that anyway.

Mai had helped broaden his perspective, parting the dense fog that had been blinding him.

They still couldn't see the road, the street signs, or the scenery around them, but by staring real hard at his feet, he felt like they could take one step at a time.

That was how Kaede was moving forward.

"Thanks, Mai. For thinking of her."

"You're welcome. I'm partly responsible here."

Kaede had wanted it, but Mai's actions had directly led to this fever. Naturally, Mai couldn't just let it go. But that wasn't the whole story. Anyone who knew Kaede's situation would hesitate before even offering to help her practice talking on the phone. And seeing her collapse as a result of that would make it even tougher to take the next step. Most people would be afraid to keep going.

But Mai was choosing to involve herself with Kaede, fully aware of what she was getting herself into. That fact alone delighted Sakuta, and her help was a real source of comfort.

"Don't push yourself, Sakuta."

"Mm? Am I?"

He hadn't expected her to shift this to him.

"Watching over something like this can really wear you down," Mai said.

"……"

"Kaede trying to change is undoubtedly a good thing, but this likely won't be the only time it leaves her running a fever. I don't think she'll get through this unscathed. Seeing her go through that can take a bigger toll on you than experiencing that kind of hardship yourself."

Mai really got it. When she and Nodoka had swapped bodies, she'd carefully avoided saying too much, maintaining the right distance—and that meant her words carried a lot of weight. Unless absolutely necessary to intervene, Mai had respected Nodoka's wishes and watched over her from a distance.

All despite the fact that she must have been deeply worried. No matter how much she wanted to say something, she'd chosen to hold back, believing that would be better for Nodoka.

"I'll be fine," he said.

"Really?"

"If it gets tough, I'll just make you pamper me."

"Well, if that's all it takes…"

He'd expected her to be mad at him, but apparently she was on board.

"Really? You're cool with that?"

"You're my boyfriend. Why wouldn't I be?"

There was a mischievous edge to her voice. The sound tickled Sakuta's ear.

"Wow, I wanna come over right now."

"Nope. I'm about to take a bath."

"That just makes me wanna come over more."

"Not today. I think Kaede has more news for you anyway."

"She does?"

That sounded like Kaede had filled Mai in on something.

"You should hear it from her."

"Huh."

He had no idea what that could be.

"So good night."

"Oh, right, good night," he said, purely on reflex.

She hung up. Mai was off to enjoy her bath. He took a moment to imagine that and then put the phone back on the hook.

The moment he did…

"Sakuta! I did it!" Kaede was leaning forward, almost grabbing him.

She had her notebook clutched to her chest again.

"That's great to hear."

"It is!"

"Great, but…what did you do?"

"This!"

Kaede hummed a fanfare and opened the notebook for him to see.

He read the page from top to bottom.

1. *Change into cute clothes. (Cute is vital!)*
2. *Short break.*
3. *Move to the front door.*
4. *Short break.*
5. *Put shoes on.*
6. *Short break.*
7. *Fuse to Sakuta's back.*
8. *Charge Sakuta-energy.*
9. *Then step outside with Sakuta. If I collapse, have Sakuta carry me back inside (princess-style!).*

He wasn't sure which part he should react to first.

At the very least, this was clearly a strategy to go outside, but... there was a lot here.

"I even came up with a backup plan in case something goes wrong!"

"Mm, that's important."

"Very!"

It seemed highly likely he was going to end up with her slung across his arms like a princess.

"It's perfect!" Kaede said. Where was this confidence coming from? That was an eternal mystery, but he was pleased to see her so motivated. With that in mind, he choked back any protests. Mai had just been talking to him about the importance of watching over Kaede's efforts.

He saw a ton of potential problems here, but...

"A flawless strategy," he said, giving it his approval.

"Flawless!"

Her smile showed no signs of doubt at all. Pure and innocent. Staring at that smile, Sakuta started quietly considering how to have Mai console him afterward.

3

The next Saturday, Kaede's fever was finally gone.

A rock solid 97.7 degrees. The bruise on her arm was gone, too. Thankfully.

Sakuta had midterms for the first three days this week, so over the weekend, Mai helped him study. When she came over, she arrived with armfuls of hand-me-down clothes and turned Kaede into her own dress-up doll.

This was all part of Kaede's master plan.

The first step in her notebook.

1.   *Change into cute clothes. (Cute is vital!)*

Mai was helping make this a reality.

Or rather, Mai spent most of the weekend having fun with Kaede by giving her new looks. Frankly, she didn't spend nearly enough time with Sakuta. Even if he tried talking to her, she just said, "How could I possibly stop now?" And when she did give him a moment, checking his studies just seemed like an afterthought.

Nodoka had come over with her and seemed rather jealous. "Man, I wish I could try on all her old stuff," she said.

"She doesn't give you any?" Sakuta said.

"Wouldn't fit. I'm not tall enough."

"Wrong body type, too," he muttered, scowling at a math problem.

"Was that a dig at my tits?"

"Would guys normally go there?"

"*You* aren't a normal guy."

Fair point. Sakuta *had* been talking about her tits, but he elected to obfuscate. Kaede wasn't exactly filled out up there, either, but since she was almost as tall as Mai, a lot of the clothes fit pretty well.

That weekend marked a noticeable improvement in the girl power of the Azusagawa residence.

"If you're stuck on that, I can help?" Nodoka said, peering over his shoulder.

"Mai said she'd teach me."

"She's clearly not doing anything but dressing Kaede up today."

"I guess I can make do with you, Toyohama."

"If you're gonna act like that, I'm not helping."

"Heartless."

"I hope you fail."

"All that'll do is make Mai sad."

Nodoka glared at him angrily.

But after a minute, she said, "Use this one."

She picked up a mechanical pencil and poked at the formula in the textbook, like this was a huge pain. She also wrote a similar problem for him to practice and praised him when he got it right.

"See, Sakuta, you can do it if you try."

"Isn't that true for everyone, though?"

"Do you have to be cynical about *everything*?"

Thanks to the idol's home tutoring, he was able to answer everything on the tests easily.

"Thanks, Professor Nodoka."

Maybe the whole educated-idol thing had some merit.

While he was busy acing his exams, Kaede started wearing the clothes Mai had given her around the house. This was part of her final prep before going outside. She'd spent most of her time indoors in her pajamas, so she wanted to get used to real clothes first.

It was a minor thing, but there was a point to clearing small hurdles like this.

Being in regular clothes made Kaede feel different. She had way better posture than she did when she was in her panda pajamas. It was like she was always on her best behavior.

After a whole day like that, she said, "That was very exhausting!" and promptly went to bed around eight.

But the next morning she got right back into it, fretting over what to wear that day and clearly enjoying herself.

"She gave you so many that you can't decide?"

"She gave me a lot!"

There was definitely a slew of new items he didn't recognize on hangers in Kaede's room. Sakuta had been the one who carried the bundles of clothing from Mai's condo, Santa Claus–style, so he'd known it was quite the pile, but he hadn't realized she'd kept *all* of them.

"We'd better thank her properly."

"Yes! I'll tell her over and over!"

Mai had been calling Kaede nearly every day, helping her get used to the phone. And Kaede used that to express her gratitude.

"Mai, thank you so much! I'm really happy!"

And then the third and final day of midterms arrived. He was well prepared for every subject.

And Kaede was similarly well prepared to go outside.

Sakuta had seen it coming, but the operation was set in motion on the evening his exams concluded.

He got home from work and found Kaede waiting for him.

"I'd like to go outside now," she said.

Sakuta had one shoe off, but he put it back on. He set his bag down near the entrance.

"All right, let's go," he said, not hesitating for a second.

"Yes! Let's!"

No time like the present. If she was ready, then there was no reason to let this opportunity go by. This was the best shot they had. It didn't matter that exams had worn him out or that he'd just gotten off a shift and was feeling pretty sleepy.

"The first step was to change into cute clothes, right?"

Kaede was standing on the doormat, just above the space for shoes. He looked her over. She was wearing one of the outfits Mai had given her. A long-sleeved dress with a soft curve to it. Natural colors, but a fashionable checkered pattern on the skirt portion. It came to just below the knees. There was a knit cap with earflaps on Kaede's head. He'd seen outfits like this on TV. Apparently, it was called the *mori* girl look.

He thought it was a really good match for Kaede's reserved personality.

"I've changed into cute clothes!"

She seemed to like it, too.

"And you took a short break?"

"I took a really long one."

"Then next is shoes."

Proceeding to the next step in her plan, he opened the shoe cabinet. He picked out a brown pair that would match her outfit and set them down in front of her.

Kaede sat on the step and picked up the shoes. It took her a bit, but she successfully got them both on.

But when she stood up, she kept fidgeting.

"Too tight?"

She hadn't worn any shoes in a long time, so there was a strong possibility her size had changed.

"It just feels really different," she said.

Kaede hadn't gone outside since they moved here. Wearing shoes would be a novel sensation.

She spread her arms out a little and took a deep breath. One, two, three in a row, and then she looked up at Sakuta. She was ready.

"Now I have to fuse with your back."

"Can you explain how this works?"

"Like this! Right up against you!"

She made a clinging gesture.

"Got it."

He didn't really, but he thought making her explain further would dampen her enthusiasm. It seemed like the sort of thing you'd figure out by doing. It didn't matter what "fusing" actually meant.

Sakuta turned around, putting his back to Kaede.

Like she'd said, she came up behind him and wrapped her arms around him. Keeping a tight grip on him from behind.

"We stick this close the whole way?" he asked.

It felt like she was about to put him in a suplex.

"The whole way."

Kaede's voice was muffled, her face buried in his back. Did he hear a slight tremor in it?

Her chest was plastered against his back, and he could definitely feel her heart racing. It was clearly beating way faster than his own.

They stayed like that, not moving, for three whole minutes.

"Uh, Kaede."

"Yes?"

"Is this the part where you charge Sakuta-energy?"

"I'm at fifty percent."

"How many more minutes?"

"Five."

She was very firm on that point.

It seemed best to follow her lead.

So he stood there with his sister stuck to him for another five minutes.

Partway through, he couldn't help but start wondering what the hell he was doing, but he decided not to worry about it. Some things were best not thought about.

He drove the thoughts out of his mind, and five minutes passed.

"Kaede, how we doing?"

"F-five more minutes."

"If you're scared, we can stop here for the day."

Sakuta felt like her shaking was only getting worse the longer they stood here.

"We've got your shoes on, so we could call that a success."

"N-no!"

Her voice shook, but she refused to back down. Putting a brave face on her fears.

"I am scared!"

He knew that. That was why he'd proposed a strategic retreat.

"I'm scared to keep being like I am."

"……"

Maybe he'd been wrong about why she was scared, though.

"When I think I might never change, I'm terrified."

"Ah."

"I like being at home! I don't have a problem staying here with Nasuno. Going outside is scary. Very scary, but…not being able to go out at all is even more frightening."

Her voice was a croak, like she could barely get the words out.

"Yeah. Maybe it is."

All he could do was believe her.

He wasn't about to tell her he understood how she felt. He couldn't say that, but he knew how things could get more frightening the longer you avoided dealing with them. He'd tried running away from his own problems and knew it just made things worse.

It was a small thing, but it was like that specific restlessness that came with blowing off studying right before an exam. Not studying was certainly easier, but that didn't mean doing other stuff would actually be enjoyable with something looming in the near future.

It was like that, except way worse. The anxiety was far stronger. And Kaede felt like that just being at home.

This was the source of her trembling. Of her racing pulse. Fear of being stuck like this forever was agonizing.

And the only way to free herself from that was to fulfill her wish of going outside.

"Kaede, I'm opening the door."

He was forcing it a bit, but he got the sense that Kaede needed a push now.

"O-okay."

She didn't stop him. Didn't ask to wait.

He could feel her heart leap. She was pressed so tight against him, her heartbeat felt like his own.

Sakuta was pretty tense himself.

But he reached for the doorknob, not stopping. He quietly turned the knob and slowly pushed the door open. The outside air came rushing in. He was sure Kaede felt it, too.

"Done."

"So it's open now."

He lowered the stopper, keeping the door propped in place.

"Kaede, question for you."

"Okay."

"Can you see anything?"

Based on the position of her head against his back, she probably couldn't. She was too close. He could feel the warmth of her breath, so she still must have had her face buried deep.

"I'm so scared my eyes are closed, so I can't see anything."

"Right, got it."

It wasn't even a matter of head positioning, then. If her eyes were closed, she couldn't possibly see a thing. Kaede had formed this plan on the assumption that her eyes would be closed the whole time. She'd been totally sure of that.

"Let's move slowly forward, then."

To get out the door, they had to take a small step.

Kaede's arms tightened, pulling him back.

"S-Sakuta."

"What?"

"Are we outside yet?"

"Still at the door."

He took another small step.

Kaede's feet followed.

"Now are we outside?"

"Not quite."

He took another step. So did she.

One more. Kaede's feet were dragged along with him.

Each step they took, her feet grew heavier. Like she was trying to stop him from going any farther. Her arms grew tighter, and she was shaking so hard that he was, too.

"Almost there, Kaede."

"W-wait!"

Her trembling was getting worse. No signs of it subsiding.

"U-um!"

He knew what she was going to say before she said it.

"I—I can't! It's too much. I can't take another step."

Her shaking became even stronger.

"Don't worry. I'm not going to move, either."

"We need to stop. I'm not worthy of going outside, not for another decade!"

"I don't think it'll take a decade, but I think you've done enough for today."

"No, I was a fool."

She ground her forehead into his back.

"For today, you should take a nice relaxing bath, and we can try again some other time."

"O-okay…" She sounded dejected.

He felt her heat peel away from his back. A moment later…

"W-wait…," Kaede said, confused.

"What?" he said, pretending he didn't notice.

"W-we're…" She trailed off.

Kaede looked down at her feet and then up at Sakuta.

One glance at their surroundings made it obvious.

"Sakuta, we're…"

"Outside."

Yep. Kaede was already out the door.

Only one step outside of it. The door was still propped wide open. But Kaede was standing on her own two feet, a few inches out of the apartment. This was an unmistakable fact.

"You tricked me!" she said.

"I did."

He had used the same principle as getting someone to ride a bike without training wheels. This was how she'd learned to ride a bike when she was a kid. Their father had held the bike upright until she could keep her balance on it. Kaede kept saying, "Don't let go, don't let go!" and he'd kept saying, "I won't, I won't," but he'd already let go. And when she pedaled, she'd swept forward without him laying a finger on it.

It was easy if you didn't know.

Kaede was a bit too timid and tended to inflate her problems.

But Kaede could step outside as long as she didn't know what she was doing.

She just didn't have the confidence to do it herself.

And this little lie would help give her that confidence.

"I—I…"

She swayed and sat down heavily.

The shock had knocked her feet out from under her. Her face crumpled up, and she started to cry.

Kaede let out a wail like a startled child.

"W-whoa, Kaede?!"

Sakuta had not expected this, and it shook him.

"Wahhhh!" she sobbed.

"Sorry, I shouldn't have lied," he said, crouching down. He stroked her hair and rubbed her head.

She threw her arms around him.

"Wahhh… You… Sakuta, you just…"

"Yeah, I'm sorry."

"No…no…"

She said that several more times, unable to think of any other words.

"No, what?"

Her sobs were almost like hiccups, but she tried to choke back her tears. Without much success. She couldn't get the words out.

"I… Wahhhh…"

"Mm."

"I'm outside…"

"Mm."

"I'm so happy I went outside. Wahhhhh!"

A new flood of tears burst out of her, and Sakuta rubbed his nose, fighting off his own tears.

4

The next few days were filled with good things.

Having managed a single step outside, two days later Kaede successfully made it as far as the elevator, and four days later to the front doors of the building.

Each new success left her feverish the next day and with fresh bruises on her arms and legs. But Kaede would recover after a day's rest, and then she'd announce herself ready to venture farther out with a smile.

Every bit of progress helped build her confidence.

Kaede's smile made that clear.

Two days ago, they'd gone to Mai's house for dinner. Yesterday, they'd gone all the way to the park.

None of these things were remotely possible without Sakuta accompanying her, but she was now walking under her own power, looking straight ahead.

Strangers were still terrifying. If they brushed past a building resident in the hall or encountered a passerby in the wild outside, she'd get very tense. If their eyes actually met, she'd shrivel up and ask to go home immediately.

Without fail, those encounters always resulted in a fever and a new bruise.

So Sakuta was unable to celebrate unreservedly. The situation required close monitoring. But it was also true that Kaede wanted to go out, and she managed longer trips each time.

That was all it took to make Sakuta happy. He was aware that he might be a bit too giddy. Frankly, he was in the sort of mood that he wished everyone around him could feel as well.

And it was all because of Kaede.

Friday, October 31.

After classes ended, Sakuta swung by the science lab to share his joy.

He planned to give Rio a full report on Kaede's progress, whether she was interested or not.

He monologued for a good ten minutes, and when he finally took a breath, the first thing Rio said was…

"Azusagawa, you've added a sister complex to your list of obscene accomplishments."

"Hardly."

That term was deeply associated with someone else in his mind. Nodoka had more than enough sister complex to go around.

"For a boy your age to talk this much about a sister two years younger is definitely diagnosable."

"You think?"

"The fact that you aren't even aware of it is proof." Rio sighed. "Although the prevailing circumstances do make it rather unavoidable."

"Yep."

After all, Kaede, of all people, was going outside. And of her own free will to boot. She was setting goals, concocting strategies, and pulling them off. What kind of brother would he be if he wasn't happy for her? Only a demon or monster would feel any other way.

"So, uh...good for her. I mean that."

"You should come over. She'd like to see you again."

"Really?"

"She said it's amazing how you know everything."

Over summer vacation, Rio had wound up staying at Sakuta's place for a while and had a fair amount of contact with Kaede. While helping her study, Rio had told her a lot of interesting science facts.

"If I feel like it, then," Rio said, acting all distant. But he could see a smile forming at the corners of her lips.

Rio had been writing something on a sticky note this whole time. When she was done, she peeled it off and stuck it on a panel she had lying on the lab table.

"A display for the culture fest?"

It was October 31. The culture festival was three days off. Every class was scrambling to get ready.

"Obviously."

The poster-sized panel was a detailed description of her experiment results. She was using sticky notes as the headline.

"Put this on the back shelf," she said, handing it to him.

"Gotcha."

He stood up, carried it to the back, and set it down where she said.

"Five inches to the right."

How exacting.

"It's off-center."

"......"

He straightened it out.

"Good enough," she said.

Slightly cross with her, he came back to his seat.

"Thanks," she said and slid a cup of coffee across the lab table. In the usual beaker. This was more than enough to make him forget why he'd been annoyed.

As he wet his throat with bitter black extract, he glanced around the lab. There were multiple panels depicting experiment reports all along the walls, maybe twenty in total. Rio was the only member of the Science Club, so this was an impressive amount of work.

He said as much, but Rio simply replied, "When there's only one member, the need for results only grows larger."

He'd heard before that the club was constantly on the verge of being shut down. Normally, clubs required a minimum of five members. The Science Club was one of those preexisting clubs where the membership had dwindled and was now barely hanging on.

"People come see this?"

Honestly, it didn't seem like the sort of thing high school kids went for. Certainly not in the throes of culture fest excitement. It reeked of academia.

And the science lab location was a problem, too. It was way off down the hall, so it would be hard to rely on incidental foot traffic.

"Several people came last year."

"One of them being Kunimi?"

"He was the only one who read every panel."

"He drives me crazy sometimes."

"Oh?"

"Everything he does is so damn charming."

"Not arguing that one."

"Naturally."

"But you were the one who stayed the longest."

"I did?"

"I know you remember."

"……"

"Well, in your case, it was more like you had nowhere else to be." For someone ostracized within their own class, and who had no friends to walk around with, what was there to do at a culture festival? In his opinion, educational practices ought to be more accommodating of students with differing social needs. It was important to learn how to handle group work and communal activities, but sometimes the best way to be cooperative was to know when to stay the hell away.

"But you're looking forward to it this year, right?"

"Mm?"

"You've got Sakurajima."

"Yeah, but that's just gonna attract an unhealthy amount of attention."

"After you asked her out in front of the whole school, suddenly that's a problem? And after she talked about your relationship on television? I'd have thought you were numb to it by now."

"Those photos were blurred out, though."

Not the ones online, mind you…

"Right, speaking of Sakurajima…"

"What?"

"And since you're dealing with Kaede… You tell Sakurajima yet?"

Rio's whole tone had changed. She was giving him a grim look through her spectacle frames. Her worry for him was clearly visible.

"About what?"

"About Kaede. That whole story."

The weight she put on those words made it very clear what Rio meant.

"……"

"So you haven't."

"I thought it was better to keep things the way they are now."

"Well…maybe you're right. If she knew, she might start treating you differently."

"Mai would probably still act naturally, but…"

Mai was a professional actress with a lifetime of experience. If she wanted to lie, Sakuta would never see through it.

"I'll tell her when the time comes."

"Okay. Then we'll leave it at that."

"Thanks for worrying, though."

"I don't want you coming to me when you have a fight, is all."

Sakuta laughed, but he genuinely couldn't tell if Rio was joking.

5

The temperature dropped quickly as November arrived. It sure felt like winter was almost here.

Every student was wearing their uniform blazer now, and athletes wore their tracksuit jackets, too.

The leaves at the park had been green not long ago, but now they were well into autumn colors. The foliage on the overeager gingko and zelkova trees was already starting to fall in the chilly breeze.

November 3. Culture Day.

And the day of Minegahara High's culture festival.

Junior high Shouko came, so he showed her around the school.

"You really *can* see the ocean from the windows," she said, sounding very impressed. "It would be nice if I could attend here."

This last bit slipped out unchecked. It hit Sakuta pretty hard. He was well aware she had a serious heart condition. The doctors had not given her long to live. It was already an open question if she'd finish junior high.

"Oh, I bet I'd spend so much time staring out the window, I'd never pay any attention in class."

Shouko laughed. No trace of tragedy on her face. She was picturing herself in high school, with a wholehearted smile.

"That's what I do. I never listen to the teachers and I'm doing just fine."

"You should really pay attention," she scolded, like an older sister.

"Yeah," he said. "I know where I wanna go to college, so it's time I started putting in the work."

"You do? Oh…even if I can pass the Minegahara exam, you'll already be gone."

She looked momentarily crestfallen.

"Assuming I don't end up getting held back a year."

"S-Sakuta! You *have* to graduate." She was suddenly very intense. Must not have sounded like a joke.

He also spent some time walking around with Mai, dropping by Tomoe's haunted house and fake screaming, checking out Rio's exhibit, and generally whiling away the time.

Tomoe had been worried about the ugly mood in her class, but with the help of her friends, they'd managed to get through it okay.

"There's still some tension, so it's a temporary fix, but…"

"All the tension in my class is centered on me, so you're doing just dandy in comparison."

"That sounds bad."

"Just what Kunimi's girlfriend told me when they were planning their flea market thing."

"You really are something, senpai."

"I think the one worthy of such praise is Kunimi's girlfriend. Takes a lot of guts to say stuff like that to someone's face."

"It's amazing you can provoke a classmate to go that far."

His verbal spar with Tomoe ended in a tie.

The only other thing of note was when he got mixed up in a little trouble stemming from the beauty contest the sports clubs took turns putting on every year. When that was over, it was basically the same as last year.

And with the festival come and gone, the school went right back to normal, with no noticeable lingering aftereffects.

Bands thrown together at the last minute in the hopes of getting girls broke up just as quickly. Some of the couples who hooked up during the excitement seemed to be making it work, but that was about it.

After a week, no one even mentioned the culture festival. They had new stuff to talk about. It was an age where gimmicky comedians were forgotten in three months.

Sakuta spent the time as always, helping Kaede with her training.

Ten days into November, Kaede's range was rapidly expanding. She'd made it all the way to the Enoden Ishigami Station just one day earlier. Fujisawa Station was closer, but they'd avoided that— three lines went through that station, and it was a big place, with far too many people going in and out.

As they watched a train pull into Ishigami Station, Kaede said, "If we take that, can we reach the water?"

She sounded exited by the prospect.

"We can."

"I'd love to see the ocean!"

"You wanna go?"

"T-today I'm ready to go home."

Her eyes had briefly met a disembarking passenger's, and she suddenly clutched Sakuta's arm.

"Sure thing."

They turned back. But Sakuta felt sure Kaede would see the ocean before too long.

And he was right.

Six days later. November 16. Sunday. A sunny day. ·

Sakuta and Kaede boarded the Enoden at Ishigami Station. The car was even emptier than he'd expected.

They were headed into winter now, so maybe the tourist trade was moving away from Enoshima and the beaches nearby.

He and Kaede found empty seats and sat down.

Even while seated, she stayed locked to his arm. She was keeping a close eye on the middle-aged women opposite them and a group of college girls near the door, as wary as a frightened animal.

She accidentally met someone's eyes and asked Sakuta, "Do they think I'm weird?"

He heard this question almost every time they went out. Kaede was very concerned about the looks they got.

"You're fine."

"But everyone keeps giving us these weirdly warm looks!"

"Because you're clinging to my arm like a koala."

"But if I let go of you, I'll die!"

The desperate tinge to her voice made it impossible to respond with a joke. She was dead serious. Her arms tightened, refusing to let go of him.

"Then just let them warmly watch over you."

"Okay. I guess warm is good."

The train reached Enoshima Station. About half the passengers got off, but just as many got on.

Among them was a group of junior high school–aged girls, in uniforms despite it being the weekend. When she saw them, Kaede hugged Sakuta's arm doubly hard.

She made herself very small, not letting herself meet anyone's eye. She seemed to have extra trouble with girls her own age. They were wearing uniforms and going to school every day, but Kaede couldn't do that. Not yet anyway.

Maybe not being able to do what everyone else could was harder than he could possibly imagine. This was the most scared she'd been all day.

They sat very still as the train stopped at Koshigoe Station and then pulled out.

"Kaede, take a look out the window."

He pointed over their shoulders. It would be a waste not to see the view the Enoden offered.

"Why?"

"Trust me."

Nervously, Kaede turned around and peered through the window.

A moment later, the train stopped weaving its way through rows of houses and came out onto the coast.

Kaede let out an almost silent gasp. Her mouth opened wider, but no sound emerged. It was a sunny day, and the light was glistening on the water's surface. And the fall skies were incredibly blue. The line dividing the sea and sky took on an almost mystic quality.

"Th-the ocean," she squeaked. Her hand tightened on his shirt sleeve. Not the most dramatic display of emotions, but there were clearly a lot running through her right now. And she was savoring all of them. That made her reaction feel that much more real. The greater the impact, the longer the silence. Sometimes the feelings rushing through you were beyond mere words.

Entranced by the sight of the sea, Kaede didn't take her eyes off it until they reached Shichirigahama Station. Her eyes gleamed as bright as the water's surface.

"Mind the gap."

Only a few others got off with them at the same stop. Once the beach season ended, few tourists came this way on weekends.

"What's that smell?" Kaede asked, blinking.

"That's the sea breeze."

"The ocean has a smell?"

They crossed a bridge and headed toward the coast. They could see the water stretched out before them.

Sakuta and Kaede walked down a gentle slope, hand in hand.

They got stuck at Route 134.

This light always took forever.

"Oh!" Kaede said, spotting something.

There was someone waiting for them across the street. Mai had just come up the stairs to the beach.

She waved at them.

When the light turned green, Kaede let go of Sakuta's hand and went running over to her. Sakuta followed her at a walk.

"You got on the train and everything? Good job," Mai said, patting Kaede's head. "As a reward, I made some lunch. Let's all eat together."

Mai lifted the basket in her hand to show Kaede.

"Wow! But why are you here?" Kaede asked, tilting her head to one side.

"I wanted to visit the beach with you," Mai explained.

If they rode a train together, Mai would attract a ton of attention, so they'd agreed to meet on-site.

"I'm glad you're here, Mai!"

Kaede took Mai's hand, and they went down the stairs together.

"Heeey!" A blond girl waved at them from the beach below.

"What, you're here, too, Toyohama?"

Sakuta had arranged things with Mai, but she hadn't mentioned Nodoka.

But having more allies was a good thing. Kaede would feel safer this way, so he was glad she'd decided to come.

Mai must have decided it would be helpful. And Nodoka had answered the call when she asked.

"Not that she'd ever turn down an invite from Mai...," Sakuta muttered under his breath.

Nodoka's sister complex would never allow it.

Onigiri taste extra good outside!" Kaede said. They had settled on a blanket, watching the waves roll in. She was smiling, her mouth full of rice. The picture of happiness. If he was asked to draw the concept of joy, this would be it.

"Mai makes the best *onigiri* to begin with."

"I made the salmon ones, actually," Nodoka said.

Sakuta quickly checked the one in his hand. Salmon pink inside. He didn't really need to look; the flavor and texture had been unmistakable…

"Ah, I was just thinking this one wasn't very—"

"Then don't eat it."

Nodoka reached out to grab it from him, but he dodged, shoving the rest in his mouth. He chewed a minute and then swallowed it all.

"……"

Nodoka scowled at him the whole time.

"The *onigiri* is innocent," he explained.

"You have any defense here, Sis? Your boyfriend has a sick personality."

She'd clearly given up this battle and was turning to Mai for help.

"When Sakuta talks like that, he just wants attention, so it's best to ignore him."

"Oh, that explains it."

Mai understood Sakuta well.

"You know me through and through, Mai," he admitted reluctantly, but the wind snatched his words away.

When they finished eating, they made sandcastles and raced along the edge of the surf, getting their digestion moving.

Since Mai and Nodoka were both here, Kaede was able to relax and enjoy herself.

Her voice raised in excitement.

And so when it was time to go, they were faced with a problem.

"Oh no!" Kaede said. She was sitting on the blanket, looking up at him, brow furrowed. At a total loss.

"Mm? What?"

"I think…"

"What?"

"I'm really tired."

"Oh."

"I don't think I can walk."

"You don't really get much exercise, huh?"

She had no way to build endurance. Too long cooped up indoors, unable to leave.

"So now what?"

A day trip ended when you got home.

"What do we do?" Kaede asked.

He could only think of one thing.

"Wanna ride?"

"Piggyback," she said, nodding gravely.

"You serious?"

"I absolutely am."

He'd been joking, but Kaede seriously didn't seem to have the strength to stand. Plus, the gleam in her eyes said she was hell-bent on getting a piggyback ride home.

He felt like he could manage to get her as far as Shichirigahama Station, so he knelt down with his back to her.

"Climb on."

"Yay!"

Her arms circled around him.

"Heave ho."

He hefted her up.

Mai had watched this whole thing, shaking her head. Nodoka seemed impressed for all the wrong reasons. "Wow. Who has the sister complex now, huh?" she said, making sure he could hear.

He pretended he hadn't and started walking up the beach.

Kaede's weight made it even harder to walk in the sand. Each time he moved a foot forward, the other sank deep.

This was tougher than he'd expected.

Mai was walking next to him, unconcerned.

"Sakuta," she said.

"Mm?"

"What's it like to flirt with your sister while your girlfriend's watching?"

"Awkward."

Mai poked him in the cheek. A cruel blow for a boy struggling to carry someone. And since he was forced to keep both hands underneath Kaede, he couldn't even fend Mai off.

But he managed to reach the base of the stairs.

The shifting footholds on the beach were bad, but this was where his real troubles began.

To get to the station, he had to climb these stairs.

And as he stepped onto the half-buried first step, a surprised voice came from above.

"Huh? Kae?"

Sakuta looked up reflexively. A girl was standing maybe twenty steps above, halfway down. Her mouth wide open.

"You know her?" Nodoka asked, reacting first. Mai whispered something to her—Mai had met this girl, too. At the Minegahara gates. They'd talked a bit.

Someone from another life.

Her name was Kotomi Kano.

And Kotomi's eyes were looking over Sakuta's shoulder—right at Kaede.

"Kae," she said again.

The same name she'd always used.

"……"

Kaede didn't answer. But she slid down off Sakuta's back.

He could feel the stress in her breath on his back.

Her hands clutched the fabric of his shirt.

"Kae?"

Kaede flinched. Kotomi was staring at her, puzzled. An obvious question rested in her eyes—why was she reacting like this?

"It's me," Kotomi said, clutching her hand to her chest, as if trying to banish the uncertainty. Her eyes were pleading for some sign of recognition.

But what came out of Kaede was probably the last thing she expected.

"Who is she?" Kaede asked. She kept hiding behind Sakuta, hackles raised.

"......?!"

Kotomi looked shocked. Her eyes fluttered. Her lips shook. She tried to speak, but nothing came out.

"S-sorry, I don't...," Kaede whispered.

"It's me! Kotomi Kano! Kae...you don't remember...?"

Kotomi leaned forward, like she was clutching at straws.

"I'm sorry," Kaede said. That was all.

He'd known this would happen if they met. This was why he'd advised against it. He'd known this would be hard for Kotomi.

"......"

Kotomi said nothing else. What was there to say? The truth left her reeling. She clearly couldn't figure out what was happening. Her face had twisted in fear.

Kaede fell silent, too. She was completely hidden behind Sakuta now.

"What's going on?"

A simple question, entirely appropriate. Mai had watched all this in silence but apparently decided it needed to be asked.

He slowly turned back toward her.

"......"

She was waiting, looking grim.

He'd known he would have to explain this one day. He just hadn't thought it would be today. But he'd been prepared for it.

He inhaled, long and slow, taking a deep breath.

And then he spoke the truth, loud enough for everyone to hear.

"Kaede has no memories."

His voice carried over the sound of the sea breeze.

Chapter
3

LIVING a DReam You
can't wake up From

1

It all started two years ago.

"We believe Kaede Azusagawa's symptoms are a form of dissociative disorder."

The diagnosing psychiatrist was a woman in her midforties. Sakuta was there with his parents when she offered up this unfamiliar term.

"Dissociative?" his father asked.

"Yes. A dissociative disorder," the psychiatrist said, writing the word on a nearby notepad.

"Huh…"

"Ordinarily, we define 'ourselves' as an amalgam of our sensations, consciousness, and memories, right?"

"……"

His parents nodded silently. Sakuta said nothing, waiting for her to continue.

"Dissociative disorders refer to cases where that identity is lost. In other words, one or more parts of that identity—your perceptions, consciousness, or memories—no longer feel like they belong to you."

"…Okay," his father said. It was only for the sake of saying something, anything.

"Common symptoms include losing sensations in part of your

body or feeling like the events unfolding in front of you are from a movie or TV show. Likewise, there are patients who suffer loss of memory. Like Kaede does."

She paused to allow them to digest this.

"It's difficult to pinpoint the exact cause, but dissociative disorders are often the result of extreme stress or psychological trauma. In other words, they're the result of a burden that's too great for the patient to bear."

"......"

None of them were capable of responding.

"Kaede had difficulty fitting in at school and has a history of self-harm, right?"

This was totally wrong, but Sakuta didn't try to correct her. He knew nobody would believe the truth.

"And she's refused to go to school since."

"Yes."

"It would be premature to identify that as the sole cause, but it's likely that those struggles put a lot of pressure on Kaede, to the point where she was no longer able to process the feelings inside her. Her suffering grew so extreme it was crushing her...and to escape that, she cut out the unpleasant parts of herself."

"...And that's the dissociation?"

"Yes. Kaede felt like she was falling apart, and this is how she protected herself."

"......"

This wasn't something they could just *accept*.

"I'm sure this all comes as a huge shock. But cases like this are not that unusual."

"So, then...Kaede is...?"

His father was looking for a solution. A way to understand what had happened to his daughter. Sitting next to him, Sakuta sympathized.

"The severity of these disorders varies for each individual. Based on what you and Kaede have told me today, what I can say now is that she seems to have lost all memories of herself, her family, her friends, and the people around her. As well as her location—she was not sure what city or prefecture she was in."

"S-so…Kaede is sick?" his mother asked. This question seemed out of place, but Sakuta had been wondering the same thing. Was this a disease?

It was nothing like what he thought of as "sick." No fevers, coughs, or runny noses.

It was more like the "amnesia" he'd seen on TV.

He'd never imagined something like that happening so close to home. He'd never even thought amnesia was actually real. In his mind, it was something that only existed in fiction. A fake disease invented to make stories more dramatic.

That made this meeting feel like a scene from a TV show. He was really impressed that this psychiatrist was getting through this exposition dump without stumbling over her words.

"It is a mental illness."

"Mental…?" his mother echoed, looking lost.

"Yes. As I've explained, Kaede has no memories of the time she's spent with the three of you. She has no access to the memories that allow her to identify you as her family. This may be difficult to understand at first, but memories are a major pool of information that form the foundation of a personality. With those memories lost, Kaede is still Kaede, but she may not be the Kaede you know. For her sake, you need to come to terms with that."

No matter how many times she said it, it just sounded crazy. For a lady in a white lab coat to be saying something like this with such a serious look on her face almost made him want to laugh out loud. But this was no laughing matter.

And he couldn't dismiss it as a lie.

When Kaede had woken up that morning, she'd forgotten everything.

She looked right at Sakuta and said, "Wh-who are you?"

Looking very scared.

And it wasn't just Sakuta. She'd done the same thing to their parents.

"What happened to me?" she'd asked.

She clearly hadn't been herself. There was no doubt about that.

"I'm sure this will be very disruptive for you, but if she is to heal, Kaede will need your help. She needs you to understand her condition and support her. We believe having somewhere safe to stay is vital to recovering lost memories."

All three of them nodded. What choice did they have?

"Understand and support." That was all there was to it. But they would soon learn that there was nothing harder.

Their memories of what she'd been like before kept getting in the way.

Sakuta and his parents remembered the old Kaede. Memories of his sister, of their daughter. Thirteen years' worth.

At first, it was difficult to even find the right distance. They knew on some level that she didn't remember them, but the expectations they had, based on how she used to be, showed on their faces. All without them being aware of it

Once, Sakuta came to see her, and he brought a book with him. A novel by one of Kaede's favorite authors. He'd seen a new release by her in the bookstore and had spent basically all the money in his wallet to buy it. For a junior high school student, 1,600 yen was a lot of money.

But he didn't hesitate. He was sure it would make her happy.

When he handed her the book, though, she seemed surprised.

"Th-thanks," she said awkwardly.

The way she looked at him made it clear she was afraid this was the wrong response.

"…Um, do I like this book?" she asked, hesitant to even do so.

It was painfully clear that the memories that defined her for him were not present. This wasn't the Kaede he remembered. Not the sister he knew. She looked the same, but it wasn't her.

And these discrepancies only grew in depth and number the more time he spent with the new Kaede.

She didn't talk the same way. She held chopsticks differently. She'd been left-handed, but now she was using her right without any problems. She ate her food in a different order. She buttoned her pajamas from the top now. Her laugh was different. She wasn't Kaede. It was all wrong, wrong, wrong…

In a matter of days, he'd noticed more than thirty differences, big ones and small ones. He'd noticed more than that but stopped counting.

It felt like continuing would drive him mad.

The differences between Kaede now and his memories of her gave him a profound sense of loss. It had taken several days for him to finally grasp that the Kaede he knew no longer existed.

And that opened a hole in his chest. An empty void. A hollow. Nothing there but the aching grief from losing something precious. An awful feeling rested in the pit of his stomach. A cloud hovered over him. Within him.

And it was on one of those days that three jagged claw marks appeared on his chest.

He was rushed to the hospital in an ambulance, covered in blood.

He still didn't know why. But he was stuck in the hospital until he couldn't bear it any longer, at which point he sneaked out of his room.

He didn't have anywhere to go.

But he couldn't sit still any longer.

He'd been unable to help Kaede when her state of mind deteriorated so much that she'd disassociated. All he wanted was to get away from that regret. The regret chased after him, so he went as far as he could.

And he wound up on the beach at Shichirigahama.

He hadn't even left the prefecture. This was somewhere he could go any time he felt like it.

But it was also a place he'd never have gone if he hadn't been running.

And there, Sakuta met her.

Shouko Makinohara.

A second-year high school girl.

To a third-year junior high boy, she'd seemed so grown-up. Beautiful black hair. The short skirt of her uniform. A face somewhere between "cute" and "pretty."' Very expressive, with a smile that was easy to like.

Shouko ran into Sakuta on the beach and decided to talk to him. He brushed her off, but she didn't give up. She listened to what he said when no one else had. She believed him.

Sakuta was past caring about the moment, the future, or the world at large, but she told him something very important.

——*"You see, Sakuta. I think living makes us kinder."*

Her words sank into the hollow left by his helplessness. They seeped into it like a sponge absorbing water.

——*"Each day, I try to be just a little nicer than I was the day before."*

This was an ideal he'd never thought of.

Sakuta had no clue what life was for, and all he'd learned in school was a canned answer, that "life" was about deciding what you wanted to be when you grew up.

About your dreams for the future.

He'd spent his adolescence with teachers and grown-ups telling him life was about finding that dream and making it happen.

Brainwashed into thinking that was what decided whether a life was worthwhile.

And he was in his last year of junior high, so his teachers were demanding he pick a high school—a simplified version of the same thing. If he scowled at his results and chose a school within his passing range, they'd nod, but if he selected something more ambitious "for his dream," they'd tell him to be more practical and pick a backup school.

Choices like that was all life meant to Sakuta.

But living to be nicer.

Nobody had told him he could do that.

The tears came streaming out because he'd felt Shouko's kindness. He knew she'd forgiven him for failing to do enough. He'd felt that…and she'd told him that he could be kinder in the future.

That was why he'd felt like it was safe to cry. And why he couldn't stop the tears.

On the way back from the beach that day, Sakuta bought a notebook and a pen. Cute ones, like girls used. He picked a thick notebook, one you could write a lot in.

Then he went straight to Kaede's hospital room.

"Kaede, I bought these for you," he said, handing the bag to her.

"What are they…?" she asked, searching his face for the right answer. Trying to read his mood. Trying to guess how "Kaede" would react while peering into the empty box of memories.

"Go on—open it."

"……"

She did as she was told.

And pulled out the thick notebook and a pen.

"Um…?" She was clearly confused. Even more lost now.

"The doctor said it might help to write. Doesn't matter what. Anything that happened, anything you were thinking about, in your own words."

Questions she had, things that made her anxious. By putting that down in words, it would help the new Kaede define herself.

"O-oh. Okay."

She didn't seem convinced. She'd lost so many memories, she had no basis to decide what was convincing. The notebook would help fill that gap.

"First, your name."

"Okay."

Kaede pulled the table across the bed and put the notebook on it. There was a space for her name on the cover, and she slowly started writing. Holding the pen all wrong. In her right hand.

"Oh, wait," he said, after she'd written the kanji for Azusagawa.

"Yes?" She looked up, blinking at him.

"About your given name."

"Don't worry, I know the kanji. *Ka* is *flower*, and *Ede* is *maple*, right?"

Sakuta shook his head.

"......?" She looked even more confused.

"Let's make it Kaede in hiragana," he said.

"Hiragana?"

"You aren't that Kaede, after all."

"......!"

Her eyes widened in surprise. Then the tears came welling up. Big droplets rolled down her cheeks, onto the notebook, blurring the kanji for Azusagawa.

"......"

Her lips quivered. Trying to say something. But she couldn't find the words.

"Sorry it took me so long," Sakuta said. "I knew better, but...I still didn't get it."

She let out a moan. More tears fell. Her moan turned into a sob.

It was like all the anxious feelings she'd been bottling up came pouring out of her. An explosion of emotion.

Since she first woke up as the new Kaede, she'd been on edge. Unsure who she could rely on, who she could trust.

She'd been all alone with her fears.

She cried like a lost child reunited with her parents at last.

And once she'd finished crying, she wrote *Kaede* in big round hiragana on the notebook cover.

She stared proudly down at the name for a while. It seemed like she'd never get tired of it.

"Sakuta…"

"Mm?"

"You're my brother, right?"

"I am."

That was the first time he saw the new Kaede smile. It felt like it'd been a long time since he'd seen his sister's smile.

He hoped the days to come would be good days for her. He hoped she'd be able to smile like this all the time.

But reality was never that simple.

Sometimes all you needed was a chance, and everything would just work out. There were also plenty of times things didn't go that way. Kaede's situation was undoubtedly the latter.

No matter how you looked at it, there was nothing easy about losing thirteen years of memories and becoming a totally different person.

After a month in the hospital, Kaede was allowed to go home.

It was fall. The maple leaves she was named after were turning red.

From that day forward, she was recuperating at home.

She may not have required hospitalization any longer, but that didn't mean she was able to return to a normal life. She didn't remember the roads around their house at all, so if she went outside, there was a chance she'd get lost. She didn't even remember the layout of their house.

It would be a long time before she was ready to go back to school.

Her classmates all knew the old Kaede. She looked the same, but it was a different Kaede inside. And it wasn't hard to imagine what effect that perception gap would have on her. For her to go to school, they'd need everyone there to understand what had happened to her. But Sakuta was convinced there was no way they could convince the classmates who'd been complicit in her bullying one way or another to grasp something this elusive.

Sakuta's own family was already struggling to understand her dissociative disorder. They were blindly feeling their way, stumbling through it with trial and error.

Moreover, a superficial understanding would just lead to mockery and ridicule.

So once she left the hospital, Kaede spent nearly all her time at home. At first, she struggled to accept her own room, since she didn't even remember it, but as the days passed, she grew more comfortable with it.

Her expression brightened, and she smiled more. When Sakuta got home from school, she nearly always came out to meet him. And she saw him off in the mornings, too.

But the situation was always gnawing away at Kaede's heart.

Sakuta had school every day. Their father had work. But their mother was a housewife, and she was the one Kaede spent the most time with.

The more they spoke and interacted, the more reasons there were to talk about the old Kaede. The house was full of things the old Kaede had used, not to mention family photographs.

"Returning to the family home, to a place she should know well—this can stimulate the lost memories. If she feels safe there, the dissociative symptoms might abate, leading to the return of her memories. Naturally, you might not see immediate results, but I think recovering at home is best for her right now."

That was the advice the doctor had given them.

"Keeping her at the hospital is less than ideal, so let's take it one day at a time."

Their mother was simply following that advice. She meant no harm by telling the new Kaede about the old one. Besides, if the old Kaede's memories returned and she "got better," then her actions were totally justified.

But that didn't mean it was good for the present Kaede.

Every time her mother said, "Just take your time," a cloud passed over her face.

"Don't force yourself" made her look deeply sorry.

"Don't worry—Mommy's here for you," their mother said, taking her hand. But Kaede had no idea how to respond to that. Her eyes always looked lost.

Nobody wanted this new Kaede. Her parents and the doctors all looked at the new Kaede and only saw the old one. That was how it must have felt to her. Sakuta got that vibe from the grown-ups around them, too. And he hated it.

Of course he wanted Kaede's memories to return. He wanted the old Kaede back, too. But what would happen to the new one, then?

The more time they spent together, the more that thought preyed on his mind.

His sister's dissociative disorder had come out of nowhere. But what would happen if it went away? Even without asking the doctors, he could imagine.

A month after she started recuperating at home, Kaede's struggles surfaced.

When she came to meet him at the door after school, he noticed bruises on her body.

The pale skin on her arms and legs was marred by purple marks. Ugly splotches. Her body creaked—an awful sound to hear. It was just like what she'd suffered when she was being bullied.

But why?

Thinking about the cause got him nowhere. He didn't know why

Adolescence Syndrome happened. People dismissed those phenomena as fiction to begin with—at least, nobody around Sakuta believed a word of it.

Maybe the cause was the hardships and anxiety Kaede felt about her new life. Maybe this was a response from the old Kaede's mind, buried deep within the new one.

"Mom, help…," he yelled, kicking his shoes off. He took Kaede to his mother in the living room. "The bruises are back!"

He showed her arms to their mother.

But she just smiled. "I see," she said. And she kept happily folding laundry by the sunlit windows. They were packed away neatly.

Only then did Sakuta realize their mother was completely out of touch with reality.

"Don't worry, Kaede. You'll be fine," she said. Her gentle smile horribly out of place.

How long had it been like this? Maybe from the very start. Their mother had never seen the new Kaede. She'd only ever had eyes for the old one.

And when their mother turned her warm smile toward Kaede, his sister shivered and hid behind him. Her fingers tightened on the sleeve of his uniform. He saw a new bruise forming on her hand. Wrapping around her wrist like a snake, coiling all the way to her elbow.

This was definitely the same thing that had happened to the old Kaede.

The doctors who examined Kaede immediately suspected that their mother was abusing her. Sakuta was sure they never doubted it.

The proof of that was how they ignored everything her children said. Sakuta was a child. Kaede had dissociative disorder. No matter how much they insisted no abuse was happening, the doctors didn't believe a word of it.

"You'll be okay," they said, never questioning their assumptions. Their misplaced goodwill landed Kaede back in the hospital.

Once there, she refused to leave her hospital room. She was terrified of the looks she got, frightened of nearly everything.

"I'm scared of the looks in their eyes. Everyone sees the old Kaede."

"Don't worry. I see *you*."

"You're the only one. You're the only one who knows *me*."

As winter arrived, Sakuta decided to talk to their father.

He was planning to leave town with Kaede and live somewhere away from their parents.

His father didn't argue. He must have known that would be better for their mother, too. Maybe he'd been considering similar solutions. But as their father, he'd been unable to propose it himself.

"Sorry, Sakuta."

"There's something you told me when I was a kid…"

"Mm?"

"You said, 'You're a big brother now.'"

"I remember."

"I couldn't do anything to help the old Kaede."

"……"

"But this time…"

He couldn't finish that thought out loud.

"Look after her," their father said.

"You take care of Mom, Dad."

"I will."

And then Sakuta and Kaede left Yokohama, moving southwest to Fujisawa. There, they started a new life as brother and sister, with only the cat, Nasuno, for company. In a new town where nobody knew the old Kaede.

And there they still were.

2

When Sakuta finished explaining all this, Mai, Nodoka, and Kotomi were left at a loss for words.

He didn't blame them. If he'd been the one listening, he'd have had trouble keeping his jaw shut, too.

There was no way they could have known. Mai and Nodoka only knew this Kaede. They had no reason to suspect she'd lost any memories. And Kotomi had only ever met the old Kaede, so how would she have known about the new one?

There was a long silence.

Mai was the first to speak.

"Kaede, you look exhausted. I think we should stop here for today."

Her first thought was to check on Kaede. She needed rest, and they needed time to process this.

Kotomi seemed to have taken the news hard. Her face was ashen.

So nobody argued with Mai's proposal.

Kotomi didn't seem like she was moving anytime soon, so Sakuta left her to Mai and Nodoka.

"We'll take her to the station," Mai said. "Sakuta, you go hail a cab."

He wasn't about to turn that offer down here.

He flagged a passing taxi and took Kaede home.

The next morning, Sakuta was woken by a cat licking his face.

"What is it, Nasuno? Morning already?"

"Mrow."

When Sakuta failed to get up, she started pawing his bed head with her front paws. Classic cat punch.

This was obnoxious, so he got up. He yawned and stretched.

He glanced at the clock. It was half past seven. Kaede usually woke him up by now.

"A lot happened yesterday…"

He went to her room to check on her.

He opened the door without knocking and found her in bed. Facedown. But she wasn't asleep. She was trying to get up, but her arms and legs wouldn't stop shaking.

"Morning, Kaede."

"M-morning, Sakuta…"

"Are you pretending to be a newborn fawn?"

She was doing an excellent imitation. Even if she was dressed as a panda.

"I might be doomed! Every part of me hurts!"

"That's muscle pain for ya."

She'd gotten too excited at the beach and frolicked like crazy. Her body simply couldn't keep up. All the muscles she usually never used were screaming at her.

"At this rate, I can't come wake you up or see you off at the door! That would be tragic! Owww…"

Her dejection was visible through the pain. She gave up and collapsed on her bed. He put a hand on her forehead, just to be sure.

Didn't seem like she had a fever. He didn't need to worry.

Then a second later he saw a bruise on the back of her neck. He pulled her pajamas aside and saw that it ran all the way down her back.

"S-Sakuta! You know I can't move, and you're taking advantage of me!"

"I'm just taking your pajamas off."

"Th-that's the problem! You should be doing that with Mai!"

"I would if I could."

"Then I'll ask her to let you!"

"Don't worry. I'll do that myself."

Who knew how she'd punish him if his sister asked her for something like that?

"Today you'd better get some rest."

He put her pajamas back in order. That bruise was probably caused by suddenly running into Kotomi. Or maybe because he'd told Mai and Nodoka about her memories. Either way, he'd have to watch her closely for a while.

"That's really all I *can* do," she wailed.

This was an accurate analysis. So he decided he didn't need to be too worried about her.

"I'd better get to school," he said.

He left her room. He was still worried, but he thought it best to act like everything was normal. He didn't want her worrying because he was behaving differently.

"Have fun!" she called.

Seeing Sakuta go about his day like usual would make it easier for Kaede to do the same.

When he glanced through the classroom windows at the Shichi-rigahama beach, it looked different from the day before.

Perhaps it was the weather, perhaps it was the temperature, or maybe…it was just Sakuta's mood.

"This'll be on the exam!" the math teacher said, drawing a red circle around the sample derivative problem on the blackboard. Midterms had only just ended, but apparently it was already time to worry about finals.

The entire class was making faces, but everyone made sure to write it down. No matter how disgruntled you might be, succeeding in high school meant it was important to heed a teacher's friendly warnings.

The math teacher picked his watch up from the podium and strapped it back on his wrist. He glanced down at it, checking the display—just as the bell rang.

It was time for lunch, and the noise levels rose sharply. A number of students were out the doors at once. Running to get in line for the bakery truck.

Normally, Sakuta would be forcing himself to his feet to join them, but today he'd been taking notes seriously and was still finishing up.

He'd promised to go to the same college as Mai, which meant he had to study properly.

When he was finally done with his notes, he found a silence had settled over the room.

Something going on?

He heard footsteps coming his way. Familiar footsteps. They sounded confident. The sound alone was elegant.

And they stopped next to Sakuta. A shadow fell over him.

He closed his notebook and looked up to find Mai standing next to his desk.

She had a small paper bag in her hands.

All the students left in the room were staring at the two of them. The world's oddest couple—an actress so famous she was a household name, and a boy destined to never fit in after rumors of the hospitalization incident went around. Everyone was curious. But nobody was being obvious about it. They were all pretending not to care. Apparently, the school had collectively decided being interested in their relationship wasn't cool. It was an unspoken rule, one nobody in particular had invented but everyone had to obey. Read the room or face the consequences.

When Sakuta's eyes met Mai's, she said, "I made lunch." Loud enough for everyone to hear.

"……"

This was delightful news. But he had not been warned in advance that she would be making it. And Mai almost never entered the second-year class, so he was somewhat taken aback.

"Come on," she said, not offering him a choice.

Mai went out in the hall. He quickly stood up to follow her.

Leaving his notes and textbook behind.

Mai led him to an empty classroom on the third floor.

There were two desks by the windows, facing the ocean. The two of them sat down side by side, as if they had counter seats with an ocean view. The Shichirigahama beach lay before them, Enoshima on the right.

"Here," Mai said, handing him one of two lunch boxes. There were sandwiches inside. Lettuce and tomato, eggs and avocado, bright and healthy looking. And he was sure they'd taste great, too.

"Thanks," he said as he took a bite.

Mai ate in silence. She washed it all down with a gulp from a box of vending-machine milk tea. Not a word passed between them.

Not until Sakuta reached for his second sandwich.

"I thought it was strange," she said.

This gambit did not surprise him. He didn't ask what. The events of the day before made it perfectly obvious why she'd brought him here.

This was about Kaede's memories.

"When did you notice?" he asked.

He'd figured she'd pick up on it eventually as they got to know each other. Thirteen years of missing memories would come up in conversation eventually.

"The first time I set foot in your house."

"That fast?"

That was a surprise. If she'd known Kaede before her memory loss, sure, but Mai had only ever met this Kaede.

"Well, she didn't know who I was."

Mai said that like it was totally expected and logical.

"Oh…"

Sakuta had to admit it was a convincing argument.

"You tried to cover by saying she didn't watch much TV, but I still thought it was weird."

This was a reason that would only apply to someone as famous as Mai Sakurajima.

It made perfect sense. Anyone from Sakuta and Kaede's generation would know who Mai was. She was one of those celebrities who everyone could match the name with the face. Mai had lived like that her whole life. It made total sense Kaede's reaction would seem weird to her.

"And the way you two act around each other."

"……"

"It's not quite how brothers and sisters usually act."

"I can't hide anything from you."

"Nodoka's been saying you two are pretty weird, too."

"She has?"

"Kaede is remarkably reverent when she talks with you, which is glaringly obvious, but you also seem like you're always holding something back whenever you're around her."

She said this like it was Nodoka's opinion, but Mai must've picked up on it, too.

"Yeah, fair enough."

Mai was right about all of it. He did hold back a bit. Kaede was his sister, but no longer the sister he'd known. And the more he treated her like a sister, the more conscious he became of the fact that he wasn't dealing with the old Kaede. It was only natural that he wouldn't be able to act as naturally as he used to.

"You said you were in your last year of junior high when it all happened? It would be like suddenly getting a new sister, two years younger than you. It would be weirder if you *could* act normal."

Mai took a sip from the straw in her milk tea. She'd kept her eyes on the ocean this whole time, and he couldn't read any emotion from her profile.

"Uh, Mai...sorry I didn't tell you."

"It's okay. You did it for her, right?"

"Yeah, but still..."

It wasn't something easily said. It was too significant. It was the sort of information that would change how people treated her. He couldn't ask them to pretend like they didn't know, and knowing would make it hard to know how to behave around her. An accomplished performer like Mai might be able to act her way past that, but he didn't want to make her do that.

And since Mai and Nodoka only knew the new Kaede, he wanted them to always treat her like that—because that was who she was.

"The more I watched Kaede adjust to being around you, the more I didn't want to say anything. The more she started to open up to you, the more I thought, 'It's better this way.'"

"I get it. I'm not mad."

She glanced sideways: Her eyes were smiling, like he had nothing to worry about.

"I'm pleased to be dating someone so understanding," he said, relieved. He reached for the sandwiches, going for an egg one next.

"There's mustard in that," she said, just as he touched it.

What horrifying news.

"Huh?"

What did that mean? Why would you put mustard on a sandwich for a boyfriend?

Mai gave him a pleasant look. When he started to draw his hand back, she said, "You're not going to eat it?" with a smile.

"So you are mad?"

"I'm not mad."

Then why was she forcing him to eat mustard?

"You won't eat the food I made?"

That was a mean way to put it. He had to eat it now.

Sakuta steeled himself and picked up the mustard sandwich. He brought it to his lips. The powerful stench hit him before he could even taste it.

He glanced over at Mai. She looked adorable but was definitely watching his every move.

He had no choice. He took a bite.

"……Mm?"

Just as he thought it might not be so bad, a horrifying shock ran down his throat and up his nose.

"……!!"

Tears welled up. He couldn't very well spit out something Mai made, though, so he swallowed through his tears.

"Here," Mai said as she handed him his tea. Sounding worried, she added, "You okay?"

She was the one who'd gotten him in this predicament, but she sure wasn't acting like it. Her performance was very convincing.

Just to be sure, he inspected the other sandwiches. The ham sandwich looked safe, but the green one was suspicious. That was supposedly avocado. Had she secretly applied wasabi to that green squishy mass?

"That green isn't wasabi, is it?"

"Weird how well avocado and wasabi go together, isn't it?"

As if that combination was normal.

"I'm sorry. Forgive me."

"I'm not mad, and I forgive you."

"Aww."

How could she even say that?

"But I am mildly vexed."

"So you're not forgiving me."

"Have you told anyone about Kaede?" she asked.

"……"

"Did you tell Shouko?"

He attempted to remain silent, but the follow-up question made that impossible. He wasn't wriggling out of this one. She'd blocked every route of escape.

"Are you jealous, Mai?"

She stretched out those beautiful legs clad in black tights right before she ground her heel into his foot. Hard. Clearly a warning not to say the wrong thing.

"Um, I did tell Shouko. And Futaba."

"Hmm. So I'm third," she muttered, like this was all terribly dull. She picked up the avocado sandwich.

Was she going to eat that herself?

"Sakuta."

"What?"

"Say 'Ahh!'"

"A mature woman wouldn't care about something as trivial as the order, right?"

"Sakuta. 'Ahh!'"

Running completely counter to the tone here, Mai was blushing slightly. Like she was bashfully force-feeding him this sandwich. He knew she was acting, but it was, well, super cute.

That meant no matter what was in that sandwich, he had to open his mouth. Male instincts took over.

"Ah...mmph!"

She shoved the avocado sandwich in. He braced himself for the blow to come, knowing it was futile.

"......"

But strangely, the attack never came. There was just a pleasant hint of wasabi, leaving plenty of room to enjoy the avocado. It was really good.

"H-huh?"

"I would never ruin perfectly good food," Mai said, looking appalled.

What had happened with the mustard sandwich, then? On second thought, he decided bringing that up would not end well, so he choked the words down.

"Let me be very clear—Mai, you are the first girl I've ever dated and will always be my number one."

"I'm not worried about *that*."

"I figured."

Sakuta turned his eyes to the water. What was life anyway? He was in the mood to ponder that again.

"That's enough penance."

"Was that what this was?"

The mustard had been powerful, but come to think of it, he'd also gotten her to feed him, so it was a net benefit overall. He vaguely regretted not savoring the "Say 'Ahh!'" scenario more. He'd been too terrified of the wasabi and wasted a perfect moment… Such a shame.

"After you took Kaede home, I talked to her a little."

"To Kano?"

Mai nodded.

"She asked about the current Kaede."

"Mm."

She'd obviously be curious. How had Kaede changed? Kotomi was the opposite of Mai and Nodoka, and she only knew the old Kaede.

"I said she was super shy at first but always very earnest and devoted to her brother… Was that the right thing to say?"

"Yeah, no need to hide anything."

And Mai had assumed as much, which was why she'd answered Kotomi's questions.

"And then she left this with me."

Mai pulled a book out of the bag she'd had their lunches in. A hardcover novel. *The Prince Gave Me a Poisoned Apple.*

"She said she'd borrowed it from Kaede. And brought it with her, intending to read it on the beach."

Mai glanced down at the cover.

"What do you think?" she asked. "If you'd rather I hang on to it, I can."

"No, it's okay."

If this was Kotomi's answer, Sakuta was honor bound to accept it.

It took courage to give up. This was a decision worth respecting. Sometimes giving up was harder than pressing on. And that was why he felt he should take the book.

"Thanks, Mai."

"For what?"

"All the things you've had to think about."

"No problem. Anything I can do to help you, Sakuta."

"……"

"Why do you look surprised?"

"I was just stunned by how cute you are today."

He absolutely meant this, but Mai merely laughed and called him an idiot.

"That's just my default," she said nonchalantly, even though it was clear she was thoroughly satisfied.

This was probably the cutest she'd been all day.

3

After school that day, Mai and Sakuta went as far as Fujisawa Station together but split up at the end of the connecting passage—by the JR gates.

Filming was underway for the new Mai Sakurajima movie—the one she'd been promoting during the press conference where she'd addressed the rumors about their relationship.

"Aww, are you gonna be too busy to spend time with me again?"

"We're starting with all the indoor stuff on the soundstages, so I'll be home on time every day."

But that implied she wouldn't be showing up at school.

"Mm? You don't film the scenes in order?"

"Almost never. Even scenes set within the same town might be filmed at locations scattered across the country."

And unnecessarily bouncing back and forth between far-flung sets was a waste of time and money.

"I've even filmed the opening scene on the final day of a shoot."

"But even so, you can still keep your performance consistent, huh?"

Pro acting sounded hard.

"I've gotta go," she said. "Let me know if anything else happens."

"I'll call you even if nothing does."

"I meant with Kaede."

"I know."

"I'll call you if nothing happens, too."

She winked at him and vanished through the gates. Headed into the city on the Shonan–Shinjuku Line.

Sakuta headed home alone. He stopped at a convenience store to pick up some pudding. A present for Kaede, who was likely still suffering from muscle pains. The good-pudding brand had a new product, with a NEW, BETTER TASTING label on it, so he bought that.

"I'm back," he called, taking his shoes off.

Kaede normally came out to meet him, but today there was no response. Was her muscle pain so bad she couldn't move? It seemed likely.

He stowed the pudding in the fridge, dropped his bag on the dining room table, and took off his uniform jacket, then hung it on the back of a chair.

Before heading for his own room, he stopped at Kaede's door.

"Kaede, I'm hooome."

"A-augh! W-welcome back!"

She sounded flustered but in good spirits. Figuring he should take a look at her to be sure, he said, "Coming in," and opened the door.

"W-wait!" she said, a second too late.

The door was already wide open.

He'd just assumed she'd still be stuck in bed, but the bed was empty. She was standing by the closet.

"……"

But not just standing. She was frozen in an awkward pose.

"I-I'm busy changing here," she explained.

"I can see that."

It was pretty unmissable.

She had on a dark-red skirt. The one from her junior high school uniform. She'd been busy putting on a vest, the type you pull over your head—and her head was still stuck inside it. Both arms raised, frozen above her—no, they were shaking a little. Her aching muscles were making it hard to move.

This was painful to look at, so Sakuta helped her pull the vest all the way on.

"O-ow! That hurts!" she protested—but she was clearly enjoying herself. It was like how you try not to laugh when someone tickles you.

"Then stay in bed like I said. Why are you up and about?"

"I wanted to put the uniform on."

"I gathered as much."

It was clearly her junior high uniform. The winter version. Her panda pajamas were tossed on the bed, abandoned. Like a cicada shell or a snake's shed skin.

"At first, it hurt every time I tried to move."

"Yeah, you couldn't even sit up this morning."

"But I slowly started to enjoy the pain."

"I know you can just laugh off muscle pain, but hearing you take pleasure in the sensation makes me very worried about your future."

"Here I was able to go all the way to the beach yesterday! I don't want a little muscle pain to get in the way right when things are going so well. I decided I wanted to go outside again today."

She said all this with the same intonation a politician would use while reciting a manifesto in the public square.

"You mean that?"

"I do!"

She hadn't even been able to get changed on her own.

"And in uniform?"

"The uniform part is important!"

How could he dissuade her?

"I bought pudding," he said, trying a light jab.

"Yay!"

She was hooked instantly. Now he was worried about her future for a very different reason.

"Ugh, owww…"

She'd tried to throw her arms up in celebration, but they were still quivering. And the pain reminded her of what really mattered.

"Don't try to distract me!" she said with a pout.

"Don't worry," he said. "The outside isn't going anywhere."

"……"

She did not seem to believe this. "Are you sure?"

"Yeah."

"I'll be okay?"

Kaede was clearly battling her fears here. Her eyes were wavering. The roots of this anxiety ran deep.

"You'll be just fine."

He patted her head gently.

"But I didn't know the girl at the beach yesterday."

The use of the conjunction was a bit odd, but he felt like he knew what she was trying to say.

"……"

"She was friends with the old Kaede?"

"Yeah."

No point hiding it.

"Her name is Kotomi Kano. If you want to know more about her, I can fill you in."

"I…"

Kaede hung her head.

"I'm not very good with people who knew her well."

She sat down on the side of her bed, staring at her fingers.

"Same goes for me," Sakuta said.

"Huh?"

"Frankly, it's exhausting."

"…Is Kotomi a good person?"

"You'll have to make up your own mind, there."

"I'm not very good with people who knew the old Kaede well," she said. It sounded like she meant something different by it this time. "But…I'm also afraid of not knowing."

She looked at Sakuta, her mind made up.

"We met Kano before Kaede was even in kindergarten," he explained. "She lived in the same apartment building as we did, on the floor above us. Kaede and I lived on the third floor, and Kano on the fourth."

"……"

"When Kaede was little, they played together all the time. Since before they could even say each other's names. Kano called her Kae, and Kaede called her Komi."

Even after they entered school and got better at speaking, those names stuck. In grade school, it was still "Kae" and "Komi."

"And she came looking for Kaede?"

"Sounds like yesterday was a total coincidence."

From what Mai had said, she'd just come to see the beach. He had no reason to doubt that. There was no way she could have ever known they'd be there. It was nothing but a fluke.

Kaede's desire to go out and Kotomi's urge to wallow in sentiment had just happened to cross paths there at the beach. Plus, Kotomi had looked genuinely surprised to see them.

"About a month ago, something happened that let Kano figure out where I go to school. She showed up at the gates."

"To see you?"

Sakuta shook his head.

"She came to return a book she borrowed from Kaede."

"What book?"

"I've got it with me. You want to see?"

"……"

Kaede thought about that one for a while. Then she looked up at her shelves.

"Can I?" she asked.

"Sure."

Sakuta stepped out of the room and grabbed his bag from the dining room table.

Back in her room, he took the book out. He could feel the tension in his hands.

"Here," he said, holding it out to her.

A hardcover novel. *The Prince Gave Me a Poisoned Apple.*

Kaede's hand slowly reached out and took it. When she saw the cover, she got up and went over to her shelves.

Her eyes were scanning the second shelf from the top. The left side of that shelf had a bunch of books by the same author. The first one was *Cinderella's Sunday*; the second was *The Naked Prince and the Grumpy Witch*. There were two more novels also written by the same Kanna Yuigahama. Four in all.

The one on the left was her debut novel, and they were lined up in order of publication.

"I thought it was weird I was missing one."

Poisoned Apple had come out between *Cinderella* and *The Naked Prince*. She'd even left enough space on the shelf for it.

Kaede put the book where it belonged.

But as she did, something fell out from between the pages.

"…What's this?"

She picked it up. It was a Western-style envelope. A cute one, with a panda on it.

No name or address.

"Should I open it?"

Sakuta saw no reason to say no.

"Why not."

Frowning, Kaede opened the unsealed envelope.

There was a card inside—maybe half the size of a postcard.

Sakuta leaned in to look. There were a few words written on it.

I'd like to be your friend again, Kae.

There were obvious signs the note had been erased and rewritten a number of times. Like she'd struggled to find the right words, wrote something down at last, only to decide it wasn't quite right, and start all over again.

He figured the message was originally for the old Kaede. This wasn't something she could have prepared between finding out about the loss of memory the day before and handing the book to Mai.

Kaede and Kotomi had been placed in different classes in junior high, and they'd drifted apart. That was why she used the word *again*. And after all the bullying, she must have felt like there was a need to start over.

But the recipient of this message was the new Kaede, not the one she'd known.

When she gave Mai the book, she'd known it would find its way to the new Kaede. She'd given it to her with that in mind. And Kotomi had chosen to leave the note inside.

I'd like to be your friend again, Kae.

This message was for the new Kaede now.

She wanted to be friends again.

Even after hearing all of that and learning about the new Kaede, she'd found the courage to take this step. Giving Mai the book had *not* been a sign she'd given up.

Maybe this was all caused by her guilt over not being able to help the old Kaede. Maybe it was just a gesture to try to make up for the past. Sakuta didn't see a problem with that. It was much more believable than good for goodness' sake.

"……"

Kaede held the little card in both hands, staring at it, reading the message again and again.

"My friend…," she said at last.

A tear rolled down her cheek. She started crying, but only from one eye.

"Kaede?"

Kaede looked up, surprised. The tears were still flowing. Silently rolling down her cheek. But only from her left eye.

Her lips trembled. Quivering, she said, "Komi…," just like she used to.

In that brief moment, he saw the old Kaede. Sakuta's heart skipped a beat, sounding a cry of alarm. A shiver started in his feet and shot through his body.

But he wasn't even given a second to think about it.

"Kaede, did you…?" he began…

…and then all the strength drained out of her.

The card fell from her fingers, and she swayed. Then she crumpled, like her soul had left her body.

He reached out and caught her in his arms. He wound up crouching under her but managed to avoid falling over.

"Hey, Kaede?!"

"……"

No response.

"Kaede!"

She was totally limp, like an empty husk. Sakuta was left calling her name in vain.

4

He could hear sirens.

An ambulance was hurrying somewhere.

He waited for it to pass by, but it never did. The earsplitting sound was following Sakuta.

This made sense. Sakuta was *in* the ambulance it was coming from.

"Pulse is stable. Breathing regular, no external injuries. Patient is unconscious."

The EMT was briefing the hospital reception. He sounded baffled.

There was no clear cause for her condition. And that was worrying.

"Preexisting conditions?"

"……"

"She's your sister?"

The intense gaze made him realize they were talking to him.

"Not sure if it's related or qualifies, but…"

He paused a moment, worried about whether they'd understand him or not.

"Spit it out," the EMT said grimly. Any information would do.

"She has a dissociative disorder."

The EMT's brow furrowed. Probably not a term he heard a lot, and it took him a moment to process.

"Got it," he said and started relaying that to the hospital.

Kaede was taken to the same hospital they'd taken Sakuta to when he'd collapsed with heatstroke.

She was carried on a stretcher from the ambulance to a hospital room, escorted by the EMT and the hospital staff.

There was no sign of Kaede coming around. It looked for all the world like she was just asleep.

Her vitals were stable.

But that was the real concern. A number of imposing-looking medical devices were wheeled in and out to examine her...but no clear results reached Sakuta's ear.

Everyone involved appeared to be at a loss. Lots of folded arms and tilted heads.

After the initial flurry of examinations, Kaede was placed in an empty private room. She lay in bed as Sakuta stood by, helpless to do anything but watch.

Her breathing was regular. He could see her chest rising and falling.

To an amateur eye, she appeared to be sleeping normally.

He stepped out of the hospital room briefly to use the public phone to contact his father. Bad timing—he was in Osaka on business. But when Sakuta told him what had happened, he promised to take the first Shinkansen he could book a ticket for.

He was probably on board one now.

Sakuta hesitated for a minute, then called Mai, too. She must've been filming, because it went straight to voice mail. He explained that Kaede had suddenly collapsed, and he left the name of the hospital.

That was two or three hours ago.

The sound of it ticking pulled his eyes toward the clock on the side table. It was just past ten thirty PM.

Well after lights-out. There were no sounds in the hall outside. The hush of the hospital whispered in his anxious ears.

"Just...shut up," he muttered, to no one in particular. Or maybe it was a threat directed at the shapeless fears swirling around his head.

There was a knock at the door shortly after.

"Yes?" he said.

It slid open.

Mai stepped in. Nodoka was with her. They must have rushed over. Mai was still wearing her full filming makeup, and Nodoka had no makeup on at all—which was rare.

They moved quietly across the room. The door slid closed without a sound.

"How is she?" Mai asked, looking down at the bed.

"Still hasn't woken up."

"Oh…"

Mai took Kaede's hand. Nodoka leaned close, peering at her face.

"Right, Sakuta, here."

Mai handed him a convenience store bag. It had *onigiri* and tea inside.

"You haven't eaten, right?"

"Thanks."

"You might want to go get a change of clothes."

Kaede was still wearing her junior high uniform.

"Nodoka and I'll watch her if you want to run home."

She glanced him over. He was still in uniform.

"Actually, uh…could I ask you to go?" he asked, pulling out his key. "I want to be here if she wakes up."

"Got it."

Mai took the key from him. She glanced at Nodoka and they left together.

About an hour later, there was another knock. He thought Mai was back, but it wasn't her.

He opened the door and found his father and a psychiatrist. A slim man his father's age, midforties.

His father glanced briefly at Kaede's bed, then back at Sakuta.

"You mind?" he said.

He didn't step inside. Even with her asleep, he didn't want to burden Kaede.

"Something we can't discuss in here?"

"……"

Silence signaled agreement.

"Okay."

He stood up and followed them into the hall.

Closing the door behind him.

As they trailed after the doctor, Sakuta asked, "When did you get here?"

"About half an hour ago," his father said, glancing at his watch.

"I see."

"When I asked for her room number, they brought me to the psychiatrist first."

He could tell from his father's profile it hadn't been an enjoyable experience.

"In here."

He was led down the row of rooms to a corner of the nurses' station. It was like a mini-exam room.

Sakuta and his father were waved to a pair of chairs.

"What I'm about to discuss are merely possibilities. Bear that in mind," the doctor said, looking Sakuta right in the eye.

"Given Kaede's condition, I figured that would be the case."

The doctor nodded. "Honestly, until she regains consciousness, there's not much we can say for sure."

"Right."

"But it's our job to prepare for what 'might' happen when she does wake up and help her family be ready for that. This is why we're discussing potential outcomes."

The doctor was choosing his words so carefully it was starting to get annoying.

Sakuta glanced at his father, who was listening with his eyes closed.

"When patients with memory loss fall unconscious, as Kaede has, they often wake up to discover some form of change where those memories are concerned."

"…You mean?"

That could be interpreted in a lot of different ways.

"You mean she might get her memories back?" he asked, going right for it.

The doctor neither nodded nor shook his head.

"That is merely one possibility."

"What are the others?"

"It could be she'll have lost the memories she currently has."

"……"

That had not occurred to him. But Kaede had already lost her memories once before. It wasn't unreasonable to think that might happen a second time.

"Of course, it's more than possible she'll wake up in the same condition she was before passing out."

"What do you think is most likely?"

"At this stage, we simply cannot know. I'm sorry…"

"Okay…"

"I realize this is frightening, but for Kaede's sake, you need to be ready when she wakes up and take her condition in stride no matter what it may be."

"……"

Sakuta didn't know what to say. He didn't want to respond at all. Instead…

"We understand," his father said, bowing his head. "Please do what you can for her."

The doctor nodded and stood up. He walked away, leaving father and son behind.

"You all right, Sakuta?"

"I know I'm not, which is good."

"I see."

"I'm not gonna make myself ready or take anything in stride."

When Kaede woke up, she might no longer be the new Kaede. There was no way to prepare for the grief that would bring.

Perhaps she'd wake up to find she had the old Kaede's memories back. But trying to prepare himself for the joy that would bring seemed utterly pointless.

Both Kaedes mattered to him. They were both his little sister.

He couldn't brace himself against any of the potential outcomes.

He couldn't pick a side.

He simply had to accept whatever happened as it happened.

When she woke up, he'd be delighted if he felt like it, and he'd cry his eyes out if he felt like doing that. What else could he do?

"Yeah. Fair enough." Sakuta's father nodded. "Fair enough."

Dawn of an Endless Night

1

It was a long night.

The lights were out, and the hospital room dark.

The moonlight streaming through the gap in the curtains cast long shadows.

Shadows of the bed's legs.

Shadows of the curtains themselves.

A shadow of an empty flower vase.

And Sakuta's shadow, sitting on a stool. His shadow fell on Kaede where she slept.

She looked so peaceful like this. As if there was nothing wrong. He felt like if he shook her shoulders, she'd blearily go, "What is iiit?"

But Kaede wasn't waking up.

When Mai and Nodoka got back, a nurse helped change her clothes, but this failed to rouse her at all. She'd made no sounds at all. Not so much as a single groan.

A sleeping beauty they could not awaken.

A silly princess with a poison apple lodged in her throat.

"Nah, Kaede's not really the 'princess' type."

It was three AM when these words slipped out. His voice sounded hoarse. Mai and Nodoka had left at midnight, and his father had left as well, staying at Sakuta's apartment.

That was the last time he'd spoken. Nearly three hours earlier.

Kaede's chest rose and fell. Proof she was still breathing.

She looked as if she might wake at any moment and also as if she might go on sleeping forever. Maybe it looked like both were true because Sakuta had lost sight of which he wanted to happen.

People saw things the way they wanted to see them.

The doctor had said there was a chance she'd wake up and have the old Kaede's memories back.

Sakuta figured that meant she'd be the old Kaede again. Memories and experiences are a big part of what forms a person's personality. If those memories came back, what would happen to the new Kaede? The Kaede he'd lived with the last two years?

"……"

He did want her to wake up. But at the same time, thinking about what that might mean was upsetting. He found it hard to look forward to it without reservation.

He'd lived with the old Kaede for thirteen years, and he wanted her back. That was what his parents wanted, and he shared those feelings.

But the time he spent with the new Kaede was his life now. She was a part of him, too.

If he could only have one of them, how could he possibly choose?

It was impossible to pick.

And even if he made a choice, reality might not follow suit. It was pointless to even think about.

There was only one thing Sakuta could do.

Act like her big brother whether she woke up as old Kaede, present Kaede, or some totally new Kaede. That was his job.

No matter what happened, that was his only option. And since that was set in stone, he simply had to be ready.

At long last, the sky in the east lightened. The dawn of a new day.

Over the next half hour, the room grew steadily brighter. The staff had started their morning rounds; he could hear footsteps coming and going in the hall outside.

It was almost seven now.

Kaede would usually be in Sakuta's room by now, trying to wake him up. But if he didn't wake up, she'd dive into bed with him. And promptly fall asleep with her arms wrapped around him.

The morning sunlight reached Kaede's face.

He'd been watching the sunbeam as it moved steadily toward her. And when it finally reached her…things began to change.

"Mm…"

Kaede made a noise in her sleep.

"!"

Sakuta leaned forward. He meant to call her name, but no sound came out. Instead, he drew a sharp breath inward.

"Mm…"

Kaede let out another muffled groan.

"…Kaede?"

This time his voice worked.

"Kaede?" he said again.

His heart was racing so loud, he wasn't sure his voice had been audible.

There was a rushing sound in his head, like a sandstorm. An alarm was ringing, like the one at a railroad crossing.

"Mm. Mm…"

Kaede's eyes fluttered open.

Which one was it? He couldn't tell.

"Hmm…?"

Kaede rubbed her eyes blearily.

"Ugh, my arm," she muttered.

Still suffering from muscle pains?

"……"

Kaede blinked at him several times. Then she sat up and saw him sitting on a stool nearby.

"Sakuta?"

"Yeah. I'm right here…"

Was it the new Kaede or the old one? She knew his name, at least. Didn't seem like she'd lost all her memories again.

"H-huh?"

Kaede finally noticed something was wrong and looked around.

"O-oh no! Where are all my things? No, wait… Wh-where am I? I… I remember changing into my uniform, and then you got home, and… Augh! I'm in my pajamas!"

She quickly pulled the hood of her panda pajamas up.

"You collapsed in your room and were brought to the hospital in an ambulance," Sakuta said. A wave of relief washed over him.

"Did you change my clothes?!" she asked, clutching her pajama buttons and looking up at him through her lashes.

"Nope, don't worry. The nurse, Mai, and Toyohama took care of that."

"I wouldn't mind if you had!"

He pretended not to hear this.

High school brothers did not help third-year junior high school sisters change.

But that was a very new Kaede thing to say.

"You are Kaede, right?" He was already certain but had to ask anyway.

"Who else would I be?" she said, looking baffled.

"Good. Glad to hear it."

At the very least, it seemed the new Kaede's memories hadn't gone anywhere. If a third Kaede had shown up, he would definitely not be feeling relieved.

"Is there something wrong with me?"

"You're not sick or anything. I don't think."

It was tough to explain. Not just for Sakuta—even doctors who'd had to study all kinds of difficult subjects to get their license were struggling with the specifics here.

"Are you feeling all right? Is your head spinning at all?"

"......"

Kaede held up a hand, then raised it toward the ceiling. She moved her head around a little.

"I'm fine," she said.

"Remember anything new?"

"...Not particularly."

"Okay. Well, let's get the doctor to take a look at you."

Sakuta pressed the nurse call button by her pillow.

Frowning, Kaede leaned toward him.

"...Sakuta."

"Mm?"

"I think I had a dream."

"What kind?"

"I was little and learning to ride a bike."

"......"

"And you were little...and Dad was there."

"Oh."

She'd have been four or five. These were the old Kaede's memories. Why would this Kaede be dreaming of those?

"Dad held on to the back of the bike until I could ride."

He'd actually let go somewhere along the way, but Kaede didn't know that.

"Kaede, do you think you're up for talking about this with the doctor?"

Her hands clutched his sleeve.

She looked up at him, searching for answers.

"I'll be with you, of course."

"I think I can."

She seemed very nervous. This was one of new Kaede's expressions. She was very shy, after all.

There was a knock at the door.

"Come in," Sakuta said.

"How can I help, Mr. Azusagawa?" the nurse asked, poking her head in. She was in her late twenties and was the same nurse who'd helped change Kaede's clothes.

She glanced toward the bed and saw Kaede sitting up.

"I'll get the doctor," she said before closing the door.

After that, they spent most of the day running tests and having different specialists examine her. The neurologist and psychiatrist took the most time.

The latter talked to her for an especially long time. It was all about what happened right before she passed out and checking if there were any changes in her memories since waking up. He kept it light, like they were just making conversation. They spoke for nearly an hour—sometimes it felt like he was running down a checklist of standard questions.

At first, Kaede was sort of hiding behind Sakuta, but by the time it ended, she was looking the doctor in the eye.

But she still clutched him tight during the other examinations, so he ended up skipping school. Not notifying anyone there would be a headache later, so he had their father call in for him.

Their father had stopped by the hospital once after hearing Kaede had woken up. But he didn't come see her. He just listened to the results of the examinations so far and then went to work. He didn't want to stress Kaede out needlessly. Even though he must have wanted to see her...

After talking to his father, Sakuta called Mai, letting her know Kaede was awake again.

"And it's the same Kaede?" Mai asked.

He'd shared the different potential outcomes with her the night before. She knew this Kaede well enough that he thought she should be prepared if something happened.

After that, it was time for the next exam, so Sakuta wound up waiting until lunchtime to give Yuuma Kunimi a call.

He'd remembered he had a shift at work that day.

"Sakuta?" Yuuma said the moment he answered.

"What are you, psychic?"

"You're the only person who calls from pay phones," Yuuma chuckled. "And I heard you were out of school today."

"From who?"

"Well, Kamisato."

"Why does your girlfriend know I'm absent?"

"She's in your class."

Yuuma laughed out loud.

"Why would anyone bother noticing?"

"You clearly don't have any idea how much you stand out."

Saki Kamisato stood out much more than he did. She was the ruler of all the girls in class. Sakuta led a quiet, unobtrusive life and could hardly compete with her. He hoped.

"So, what?"

"Can you take over my shift today?"

"You sick? You don't sound sick."

"Nah, it's Kaede related. We're at the hospital."

"Oh, I see. Fine. Just buy me lunch sometime."

"Will a dinner roll do?"

"You mean the plain ones that are always left over?"

The bakery truck's least popular item. But because nobody bought them, people desperate for any form of lunch were still able to eat.

"Exaaactly," Sakuta said. "Thanks, though. It's a big help."

"Sure thing."

Sakuta hung up. It was nice to have friends who'd bail you out in a pinch. Made all the difference.

"Maybe I'll make it two rolls."

After the hospital examination tour concluded, Sakuta and Kaede returned to her hospital room and found the sun already hanging low in the west.

"Whew," Kaede said as she plopped down on the bed. Sakuta let out a weary sigh himself.

He'd just been along for the ride, but it had taken a lot out of him, too.

Being in this huge hospital, surrounded by strange grown-ups, definitely brought out Kaede's shy side. That meant he couldn't leave her alone. She'd clung to him koala-style through most of the testing.

The one time she had voluntarily distanced herself was when they weighed her.

"You can't watch this!"

"I'm not gonna be upset even if you're way over a hundred and ten pounds."

"N-no little sister is that heavy! It's the law of the universe!"

"Nah, at your height, it's more than possible."

He glanced at the nurse for help, but she kept her expression neutral. Girls backed each other up, apparently.

"A sister should weigh no more than three watermelons!"

"That seems plenty heavy."

Ultimately, Kaede's exact weight remained a secret for him. He didn't actually care, so that was fine, but…

Including such basic physical checkups, Kaede went through a battery of tests and examinations. The end result of all that? Apparently, there was absolutely nothing wrong with her.

The only thing that could even remotely be considered an issue was the lingering muscle pain.

In other words, she was physically healthy.

But looked at another way, that meant they didn't know for sure why she'd collapsed.

"We'll monitor her condition for a day, and then she can go home tomorrow," the doctor explained.

But Sakuta found it hard to feel relieved.

In fact, the doctor had a pretty hefty follow-up to that statement.

"The tests we ran didn't find anything out of the ordinary physically. But dissociative disorders rarely affect the results of these kinds of tests. I think it's best the family keeps a close eye on her for the time being. It's a reasonable assumption that this loss of consciousness is a sign Kaede's memories are returning. And there is a possibility that those memories returning fully will lead to a loss of the memories she's made in the meantime. Try to take the situation in stride, as a family."

And that had planted a seed of doubt in Sakuta's mind.

No, that seed had probably been lying in wait for the last two years, too. Ever since they moved to Fujisawa and he started living with the new Kaede, he'd known this moment might one day come.

But it had taken so long and so much time had passed without incident that he'd begun to think maybe they'd stay like this forever. It was a natural process.

He had no real basis for this belief, but the time spent undisturbed had made him feel secure.

But the passage of still more time had brought the harsh reality to bear. The seed lodged in his heart had finally decided to emerge from that soil.

Perhaps Sakuta's efforts to help her had caused this bud to grow.

"I believe the safety provided by her current environment has eased the symptoms of Kaede's dissociative disorder. The best thing you can do is keep going exactly as you have been," the doctor said.

What was right? What was wrong?

There was no real answer.

There was just the simple truth that he was here with Kaede.

And Kaede had been officially given a clean bill of health. She was doing *great*.

On the day of her discharge, Sakuta left school and found Kaede waiting for him impatiently.

He left all the paperwork up to their father—who'd taken the day off—and was here to take Kaede home.

Most of the trip was in a cab the hospital had called for them. But Kaede said she wanted to walk a bit, so they had it stop at the park near their apartment.

The western sun was bathing the road from the station.

They walked into the park, and Kaede sat down on a bench.

With winter fast approaching, the trees in the park were losing their autumn-colored leaves.

"Dad came?" Kaede asked.

"Mm?"

"To the hospital."

She had her hands on her knees and was locking and unlocking her fingers uneasily.

"Yeah, he was there."

"……"

"He was worried about you."

"……"

Kaede just stared at her fingers, saying nothing. Not sure how to respond. Maybe she was thinking about the old Kaede.

"Kaede."

"Yes?"

"What do you want to do now?"

"……"

She looked up at him, surprised. Sakuta turned his eyes to the sky, fleeing her gaze. The sky in the east was growing dark. Evening on its way. The west was still red. The way the red faded into the blue of the night was beautiful. Was there a word for the color in between?

"To celebrate getting out," he said.

"I want some pudding!"

"We can do something bigger than that."

"A bigger pudding?!"

"Okay, I see we're locked on pudding. But I meant, like, go see the pandas, or…"

"Oh, that kind of bigger."

She pursed her lips, considering it. Ten full seconds passed with no further response. Instead, they heard voices at the edge of the park.

Kaede's shoulders shook, and she moved closer to Sakuta. Even as she hid herself, she looked toward the street at the park entrance.

There were three girls in junior high uniforms. The same uniform as the school Kaede was supposed to be attending.

They were walking along, eating steamed buns.

"Can I have a bite of that?"

"Trade you?"

"Ugh, don't get greedy!"

"It was just one bite!"

"Get fat."

"So mean!"

They were laughing happily. They were soon out of sight, but their voices could still be heard for a minute longer.

Kaede finally peeled off Sakuta when they were out of earshot.

"Pandas are second," she whispered.

A very serious look had appeared on her face.

"And first?"

"I want to go to school."

When she said this, Sakuta felt it was unexpected.

But when he looked deep into her eyes, he realized it shouldn't have been. He'd known all along that Kaede's biggest, hardest, and most yearned for goal was going to school.

School wasn't anything special for Sakuta. It didn't matter to him. Classes were boring, exams were a pain, and paying attention to everyone's mood to preserve relationships was absolutely exhausting.

But it was part of his life and the way it should be. Classes weren't unbearably boring. Exams were only for a few days. He didn't have many friends, but he had good times with them, enough that these friendships felt worth maintaining.

That was what going to school meant. Sometimes you and your friends could go shopping or grab a bite to eat afterward. That sort of ordinary pleasure was what Kaede craved. She just wanted what was normal, to be normal. To rid herself of the anxiety that came with failing to be normal.

"All right."

"Sakuta?"

"Let's do whatever it takes to get you to school."

Kaede took a deep breath, mulling over his words. Then she smiled.

"Yes!" she said. "I'm gonna make it happen!"

2

That evening, after Kaede was in bed, Sakuta called their father.

——*"I want to go to school."*

He was taking steps to fulfill that earnest desire. This was the first step.

It wasn't easy to come back from an absence as long as hers. Kaede's feelings and readiness were important, but they also needed help from her school. If they couldn't understand what her dissociative disorder meant, they'd never get anywhere.

"Something happen?" their father asked, already worried.

"Kaede says she wants to go to school."

"Oh."

"I'd like to help make that possible."

If they weren't talking on the phone, he never would've been able to voice his feelings this easily.

He could tell his father had to think about this one. Even so, he said "Okay" before Sakuta felt the need to say anything more. "I'll call her school tomorrow, explain the situation," his father said, speaking slowly and clearly.

"Mm."

"I'll probably need to meet with them."

"I figured."

Steps like this were best left to grown-ups. If a high schooler like Sakuta rolled up, it would just make everything complicated. He'd have to start by explaining why a kid like him was handling this sort of thing. And the powers that be would most likely not accept that explanation. There was no need to waste time and effort on that.

"Sakuta."

"Mm?"

"Are you eating properly?"

That came out of nowhere.

But it didn't surprise Sakuta, either.

"I am," he answered.

He felt sure his father was really asking something else. They had no way of knowing what would happen with Kaede's memories in the future. The doctor had said they might be coming back. That her collapse might be a sign that was happening.

And that could mean the return of the old Kaede.

But Sakuta had lived with this Kaede for two years, and his father was worried about that. If something happened to her, he'd feel the loss. It would be excruciating. Sakuta might soon have to face that same devastating grief again, the grief he'd felt when they lost the old Kaede.

"Eating right is important," his father said. Knowing full well that nothing he said could change anything…so the words wound up being about something unrelated.

"I got it," Sakuta said, responding in kind.

"Good."

"Mm."

Sometimes a vague grunt was the best response.

"And…this can wait until things settle down, but…"

"What?"

"……"

There was a pause. A breath on the other end of the line. A hesitation. Sakuta wondered why, but then his father said, "I'd like to properly meet this girlfriend of yours."

"Oh…," Sakuta said. He wasn't sure how to respond, and that was definitely obvious from his reflexive reaction. Maybe that was the right response. It was for sure way too late to try to hide it.

While Kaede was unconscious, their father had rushed to the hospital, and Mai had shown up with a change of clothes for Kaede, and they'd bumped into each other. Since everyone was focused on Kaede's condition, it had been a very brief interaction.

To Sakuta's eyes, his father was always collected and calm—but in that instant, he'd been clearly caught off guard. Anyone would be rattled by a sudden encounter with an actress that famous. And someone in his father's generation would have seen her grow up on-screen. Given how much media attention her relationship had been given, finding out the boy in the picture was his son would be a shock to anyone.

"Uh, yeah…when things settle down."

He elected not to commit to anything just yet. But it didn't feel avoidable for long. After their brief meeting, Mai had definitely hinted that she wanted a more formal introduction in due time. She'd been in show business her whole life, which had made her very big on manners and proper greetings.

Sakuta wanted to avoid it at all costs. Introducing a girlfriend to your parents was even more embarrassing than showing them your butthole.

But clearly, there was no getting out of it now. He had to steel himself for the inevitable. Even if he could somehow fend off his father, Mai would not stand for it.

"Treat her right, you hear?"

He was definitely referring to Mai.

Carrying on this conversation was clearly bad for his mental health, so Sakuta thanked his father for helping with Kaede's school and hung up.

When he put the phone down, he realized he was covered in sweat.

"Well...what's done is done," he muttered.

Knowing when to give up was critical. Giving up made most things work out.

3

The next day was November 20, a Thursday. Sakuta left the house to go to school and bumped into Mai outside as she was dragging a suitcase behind her.

She'd explained she was headed out to a location shoot in Kanazawa. That giant suitcase must have been filled with all the clothes she'd need while filming. He was intrigued.

Nodoka was next to Mai, wearing the uniform of her rich girls' school and helping pop the suitcase down the step. A beautiful shot of two loving sisters.

There was a car waiting for Mai on the street outside. A white minivan. A woman in a suit stepped out of the driver's seat—Mai's manager. Her name was Ryouko Hanawa, if memory served. She was in her midtwenties and had once been nicknamed Holstein.

The way she closed the door made her seem flustered. Even getting out of the car, she'd been thrashing her legs around. Mai was much younger but far more collected.

"Good morning, Ryouko."

"Good morning. Let me take your things."

"Ah, yes, please. Thank you."

Ryouko took the suitcase, opened the sliding door, and loaded it into the back seat.

While she did this, Mai saw Sakuta and came over to him.

"Two weeks, was it?" he said.

"I'm sure you'll be lonely without me, but I promise I'll call every night."

"Then I'll wait by the phone every evening."

"No need for that. Focus on your studying instead."

"I'll be too excited about talking with you to focus on anything."

This seemed like a perfectly legitimate excuse to him.

"Don't use me as a reason to slack off," Mai said, rapping him lightly on the head.

"Can I get a good-bye kiss at least?"

"I can't do that with Nodoka and Ryouko watching."

Ryouko had finished storing the suitcase and kept glancing in their direction. Moving three steps right, then three steps left. Like an animal in the zoo. It was clear she was rather on edge.

"I really put her through the wringer dealing with the rumor mill, so I'd better take it easy for a while. Ryouko gained seven pounds from the stress."

"Doesn't stress usually make you lose weight?"

People often said they lost their appetites.

"She said sweet treats were the only thing that eased her exhaustion, so…it happens."

He glanced toward Ryouko again. She was still shifting back and forth.

"I think she could gain another seven pounds and still be just fine."

She had a slender build to begin with. He didn't see any signs that she was even the least bit overweight. Sure, she was more solidly built than active stars like Mai or Nodoka, but that just meant she was squarely in the realm of "normal."

"Once the location shoot is over and I'm back, I'll give you a kiss then," Mai said, looking up at him through her lashes, her voice soft enough that only he could hear.

This just made him want to kiss her now.

"Bye," she said with a smirk that seemed to say she knew exactly what he was thinking. She'd lit his heart on fire and then strolled away to the waiting car.

"Oh, wait! Mai!"

"What?" she said, glancing back.

"Uh, when things settle down a bit…my dad wants to meet you properly."

"Sure thing," she said with a happy grin.

"Also."

"There's more?" She blinked.

"You are super cute today."

"……"

She gaped at him. Then she started to say something, thought better of it, and decided to just flash him a wordless smile. A pleased one. She gave him a little wave and then trotted off back to the car. She climbed inside and shut the door.

A moment later, Ryouko got in the driver's seat. The engine started, and the minivan pulled away. Mai waved from the window and was soon out of sight. He waited until the taillights disappeared left around the corner, then headed toward the station with Nodoka.

"……"

"……"

Neither of them said anything at first. But it felt like she was trying to find the right timing to start a conversation. She kept glancing over at him.

It was always easy to tell when Nodoka was hiding things. She was an open book.

"What, do you need to go to the bathroom?"

"Huh? Why would I?"

"Then what is it?"

"What's that supposed to mean?"

"You look like you've got something to say to me."

Nodoka hesitated for a moment.

"If you drag this out, I'll be too busy wondering about it to focus on class, so please. Spit it out."

"You never pay attention in class."

"Actually? Lately, I'm trying my best to."

After all, he had to go the same college as Mai now.

"Okay, then let me ask—why do you look so normal?"

"Huh?"

"Aren't you scared?"

She was leaving far too much unsaid, but Sakuta knew what she meant. He'd known what she wanted to ask before she'd even opened her mouth.

This was about Kaede.

He couldn't think of anything else she'd want to ask him now.

At first, he wanted to just shrug it off. If he hadn't seen the serious expression on her face, he might have. If she'd simply been curious, maybe that would have been an option.

But when he turned to glance at her, he caught a glimpse of sadness in Nodoka's eyes. A lost look. Clearly one born from genuine concern. Concern that had come out as a question.

He couldn't just blow that off.

"Of course I'm scared."

"……"

"I might even piss myself."

"I'm being serious."

"But you can't screw up in front of your kid sister, can't you? Can't piss yourself, shit yourself, or show any sign of weakness."

They stopped at a red light.

"If there's anything I can do for her, then I'll try to do it."

"……"

"But there isn't anything I can do."

He kept his voice flat.

If there was a way to make both Kaedes happy, he'd have gone for it long ago. If there was a way to make the people around her get their bearings, he'd have spared no effort. He wouldn't even have considered it "effort." It would have been normal. Like breathing. Just the way things were.

But there was no easy solution.

There was nothing cruel about it; it was just a fact that the two of them could not both exist.

"…Sorry," Nodoka whispered.

"Mm?"

"Argh! Dammit! I'm an idiot."

She suddenly crouched down and messed up her hair.

"Don't start losing it on me, here. Everyone'll start looking at me funny, too."

To a bystander, she was just a flashy blond school girl yelling and crouching low for no apparent reason. A passing businessman gave them a wide berth, and Sakuta sympathized.

The light turned green, and the businessman quickly crossed. Sakuta followed.

"Ah, wait!" Nodoka scrambled after him. "Even after my sister didn't say anything because there's nothing you can do, I went and had to ask... Sorry."

More apologies.

She looked dejected.

"Toyohama, if your idol career never takes off, what'll you do then?"

"What kind of question is that? Too early to think about."

Nodoka scowled at him.

"Think you'll be all, 'I should never have been an idol' or 'That was a waste of time and energy'? Think you'll wish none of it had ever happened?"

Sakuta wasn't really sure what answer he was fishing for. He just...wanted to know.

"Of course not!" Nodoka snapped. There was rock-solid certainty behind her assertion.

"Why do you think that is?"

"I've met a lot of people doing the idol thing, had a lot of new experiences, felt things I never would have felt...and I mean, it hasn't all been good memories, and I know that, but...I feel like all of that, good or bad, made me who am now, I guess."

She must have grown embarrassed by her own serious tone, because somewhere in the middle she started trying to make a joke of it.

"I mean, sure, there's stuff I regret. 'I shoulda done that,' or 'I coulda done so much more!'" Nodoka said, like she was making excuses. Maybe trying to hide her embarrassment.

"Oh. Well, good."

"Huh? Good how?"

"I don't think I could be friends with the kind of positive monster who'd say crap like 'I did all I could do, so I have no regrets!' with a straight face."

There would always be regrets. The more important something is, the more it matters, then the greater the emotional investment would become...and the bigger the regrets when things don't go as hoped.

What mattered was how you dealt with those feelings. How you processed them. And from Nodoka's answer, she was already on her way.

"I guess that's it," he muttered.

"Huh? You figure something out there?"

"We're all gonna die someday, so the secret to life is to enjoy the journey, not the end. I wonder how we can tell everyone that."

"I wasn't talking about anything like that, and I sure as hell don't have any deep philosophy behind *my* life."

Nodoka rolled her eyes at him.

"I gotta think like this to get through it," he said.

Nodoka leaned forward, peering up at his face.

"What?" he said.

"You sounded like you really meant that."

Why did she sound so happy?

"But yeah," she said. "I guess I should just keep doing what I've been doing."

"Keep acting normal around Kaede as much as possible."

"I dunno if I can. But I'll try."

That was very Nodoka. For all her flashy style, she was really earnest underneath.

4

That Saturday...

After he and Kaede finished lunch, Sakuta went out alone, walking an unfamiliar route to school. Unfamiliar because it wasn't his school, but Kaede's.

Sakuta graduated from junior high back in Yokohama before they moved, so he'd never actually walked this route. Never even been down these roads. It was all new to him, but the roads looked like roads you'd find anywhere. Still felt a little novel, though.

It was maybe a ten-minute walk.

He first saw green nets above the schoolyard. As he got closer, he saw the white walls of the school building.

Her junior high.

Sakuta saw a familiar figure outside the gates. In a suit and tie. His dad was watching the baseball team practice.

"I'm here."

"Mm," his dad said. He must have heard Sakuta's footsteps approaching.

Why were they meeting here?

Simple.

This was the result of the call his dad had made to the school.

The faculty had been unexpectedly nimble, responding instantly to a proposed meeting with Kaede's guardians. Since his father had work, they set the meeting on the next available Saturday—November 22, today.

"Shall we?"

His father stepped through the school gates without hesitation. Sakuta followed. He was still feeling pretty antsy. It was always stressful entering a school that wasn't his. It felt like he was doing something wrong, a fact he found intriguing.

Just inside the entrance was the office. His father made the appropriate greetings. Everyone seemed aware of the situation. A woman in her forties stepped forward to meet them.

"I'm in charge of Class 3-1," she explained, bowing. In other words, she was Kaede's homeroom teacher. They'd spoken once at the start of the year, but so much time had passed, Sakuta had forgotten what she looked like.

"This way."

She led Sakuta and his father to a reception room between the faculty room and the principal's office. The walls were lined with trophies.

As they settled down on a couch, the vice-principal—who was already seated across from them—explained, "They're primarily athletic trophies."

Kaede's homeroom teacher sat down next to him. There was a folding chair to one side, and a familiar looking thirtysomething woman was seated on that—the school counselor.

Her name was Miwako Tomobe.

She'd been stopping by to check on Kaede once a month. Kaede called her "Ms. Miwako" on an ambiguous first-name basis, but Sakuta stuck to "Ms. Tomobe."

With everyone assembled, his father began to elaborate on Kaede's situation. What had happened at her previous school and the events leading up to her dissociative disorder. And how she had expressed a desire to go to school.

They definitely didn't seem sure what to make of memory loss from a dissociative disorder. But before the meeting began, they'd already decided how they were going to handle the situation.

"Our school will, of course, do everything we can to support Kaede's attendance," the vice-principal said, his chrome dome glistening magnificently. He smiled at Sakuta's father, then turned to Miwako. "We believe the best course of action is to work closely with our school counselor, Ms. Tomobe, to determine how to proceed."

Miwako bowed her head. "I think it's best to take these things slowly. For example, begin by walking partway to school. If that goes well, go a little farther each time, closer and closer to school. Consider the school gates her goal for a while and give her feelings time to adjust so she doesn't feel so scared of the idea of going to school. My concern is that she'll put too much pressure on herself; feeling like she *has* to go to school can sometimes make things worse."

"Right." His father nodded quietly.

"Once she's adjusted to the commute, we're thinking she can start by coming straight to the nurse's office. You said she's able to go outside now, but from what you've told us, she's still very nervous around children her age."

Miwako glanced at Sakuta, who nodded.

"The nurse's office can be a safe space to get used to being at school. At this point in time, it's best to consider the classroom a much more distant goal."

"One question," Sakuta said, raising a hand.

"Yes? Go ahead."

"Would being in the nurse's office attract undue attention?"

They weren't exactly setting out to hide a tree in a forest, but being the only person located somewhere else would really stand out. Like being the only student in class while everyone else was in the schoolyard, or the other way around. There was a reason most students hated being the only one sitting out during gym classes.

"That's a fair question," Miwako said, taking his question in stride. "There are certainly students who would find that more objectionable, so perhaps it's best to discuss the idea with Kaede before we decide."

It sounded like she'd anticipated this concern. Maybe the idea came up any time there was a case like this.

"If it's all right with you, I'd like to meet with Kaede after this and talk things over with her directly," she said, looking from Sakuta to his father.

She might be flexible, but she was quite firm on what needed to be done.

Sakuta's father looked at him.

He was leaving the decision in his hands. More than trying to shirk responsibility, he was simply well aware that Sakuta knew Kaede better. Kaede, too, was primarily reliant on him. His father knew Sakuta should be the one to make the decision.

"Can I call and check with her?"

"Yes, that's probably for the best."

His father took his phone out. It wasn't a smartphone, but an older flip phone, a simple white one.

Sakuta took it from him and found his home number in the address book.

"I'll make this quick," he said and stepped out into the hall, listening to the ringtone.

After a few rings, it went to the answering machine.

"Kaede, it's me. If you're there, pick up."

She instantly responded.

"Hello! This is Kaede!"

"Mind if we bring a guest back with us?"

"A guest?"

"The school counselor."

"…Ms. Miwako?"

"Yep."

Kaede didn't answer right away, and Sakuta suspected he knew why. Kaede had met Miwako before but hadn't really warmed up to her. They hadn't exactly gotten off on the right foot. That was maybe Sakuta's fault. He'd introduced her as the school counselor, so Kaede had assumed her job was to make Kaede go to school. Which meant she'd seen her as someone scary.

That misunderstanding had been long since cleared up, but the unfortunate first impression still lingered.

"Wh-what for?" Kaede asked, proving his point.

"Strategy planning for how best to get you to school."

"O-oh, in that case, then okay."

"You're sure?"

"Y-yes."

She sounded tense, but not like she was forcing herself.

"All right. Won't be too much longer."

"I-I'll be here!"

Sakuta waited until Kaede hung up, then snapped the phone closed.

5

It was after three by the time Sakuta and Miwako left the school grounds.

His father stayed behind, exchanging a few words with the principal (who'd finally shown himself).

"Teachers work Saturdays, too?" Sakuta asked.

"Weekdays we're busy dealing with students. That means they're usually here weekends to prep classes, et cetera. And third-year teachers have to think about each of their students' futures, which is a lot of work."

"Doesn't sound like it affects you, though."

"My role is a bit different from the teachers. I think I mentioned that this isn't the only junior high under my purview?"

Her look definitely suggested he shouldn't have forgotten that.

"Maybe you just seem like a school nurse and I got confused," he said.

He did remember her explaining this, now that she brought it up. He hadn't been sure what exactly a school counselor was, at first. In Miwako's case, he was pretty sure she had a clinical psychology degree and was employed by the board of education directly.

"Ideally, I would be in residency at a single school, like the nurse is. But lack of personnel and funds make that impractical."

"So typical grown-up problems," he said. That sarcasm was probably unnecessary.

"Oh, aren't you a spiteful one," Miwako said. "I think you need a little counseling yourself."

She said that almost every time they met. He didn't really handle her any better than Kaede did.

"Here we are," he said, pretending he hadn't heard. He glanced up at his apartment building.

"Good conflict evasion," she said.

"……"

He opened the front doors, and they waited for the elevator. Inside, he pressed the button, and it carried them to his floor.

He opened the apartment door and called, "We're here."

"W-welcome back, Sakuta," Kaede replied.

She was all the way down the hall, hiding behind the door to the living room. Only her face visible.

"Thanks for having me. How are you, Kaede?" Miwako asked, keeping her tone warm.

"F-fine, thanks." Kaede sounded tense.

She might be able to go outside, but that didn't mean she had suddenly started opening up to Miwako.

Sakuta led Miwako into the living room, and Kaede retreated to the far corner…then swung around and hid behind Sakuta.

But there was one clear change in her behavior from earlier Miwako encounters. On all previous occasions, she'd been in her panda pajamas, but now she was wearing her junior high uniform. She'd left her door half-open, and he could see the cast-off pajamas on the floor.

She must have quickly changed when he called. But she only had one sock on, so she must have run out of time.

"The uniform looks good," Miwako said, smiling. Not at Sakuta, but at Kaede.

Kaede peeped around his back.

"Th-thanks," she said softly.

But Miwako heard her. "Sure. Let's talk strategy, shall we?"

Sakuta waved her to the dining room table. Miwako sat on the edge of a chair and began explaining what Sakuta and his father had discussed at school.

How she should take it one step at a time.

Starting with just walking to school.

How just making it to the gate was enough.

And then the suggestion that she could come to the nurse's office.

Kaede listened intently.

When Miwako finished, she said, "U-um…"

"Yes? Go ahead."

"I—I have a question." Kaede raised a hand over Sakuta's shoulder.

"Ask anything you want, Kaede."

"Do I not have to go to the classroom?"

"Do you want to?"

"I don't want to be different from everyone else."

That was a bit disconnected from the question. But it went straight to the heart of the matter. The point of this meeting was to feel out what Kaede thought she could and couldn't do.

"You'd rather be with everyone else?"

"I'm afraid…of them all staring at me."

"So which approach seems easier?"

"……"

Kaede had to think about that for a while.

"I think…," she said, "that I'm most afraid of having everyone looking at me."

"Well, being in the nurse's office will put some distance between you and the other students. It might be worth starting there."

"…Er, um…"

Kaede raised her hand again.

"Go on."

"D-does the nurse's office count as going to school?"

She sounded extra tense. And not because talking to Miwako was stressful. There was an added note of desperation.

"Yes, of course it does," Miwako said firmly.

"B-but…that's not what everyone else is doing."

"That's true. But even if they seem the same, everyone is actually different."

"…They are?"

Kaede leaned to her right quizzically. Pulling Sakuta with her.

"For example…one girl might be tall, while another is short. One kid might be good at running, but another one not so much. Like that, there are children who easily adapt to being at school and children who struggle with it."

"……"

"I wouldn't tell short girls to get taller. They can't do that. Everyone has to take things at their own pace. We have different ways of doing things, different ways of living. School is a very rich environment that can help you learn social skills and how to get along with other people, but sometimes it can force you to maintain a speed you aren't comfortable with. And if we treat children who can't keep up like there's something wrong with them, then that's a problem with the teachers. It means they have a lot to learn, too, and have yet to accept how diverse humanity really is. That's how I see it anyway. Kaede, I think if you try your best, whatever results you manage should count as 'going to school.' Even if you're just going to the nurse's office, I'd consider that a triumph."

"Then can I put down a circle if I can make it to the nurse's office?"

"Circle?" Miwako blinked at her.

"I-in this."

Kaede held up her notebook for Miwako to see. Her list of goals for the year. She'd already put circles next to a lot of things.

"I think so. Right?" Miwako looked at Sakuta for approval.

"Of course," he said, nodding.

"Th-then I definitely want to go to school," Kaede said.

And so, Kaede's goal was set.

Now they just had to take it one step at a time.

Each one leading toward school.

One step forward after another.

Chapter
5

And once more,
the sun rises

1

They started practicing the trip to school the next day, Sunday, November 23.

Somehow they already only had a week left in the month. The end of the year was coming up fast.

There was a reason why they started practicing on a Sunday, when there weren't any classes. On weekdays, the road would be packed with students, but today, there were far fewer eyes on her, which was less of a burden on Kaede, mentally. Miwako had suggested trying around this time.

Also, Kaede herself really wanted to start training as soon as possible.

She was so fired up about it, she'd already changed into her uniform when she came to wake Sakuta up that morning.

Seeing that had helped Sakuta fight off his desire to sleep in, and he got up.

Kaede still couldn't go outside by herself, let alone to school, so Sakuta would have to help her practice.

After both of them finished breakfast, Sakuta got changed, too. Then they set off.

The elevator brought them to the ground floor, where they stepped though the building doors to the street outside.

No problems so far.

Well, maybe Kaede did seem extra twitchy about other people. Every time she heard a voice or a noise, she froze, hackles raised like a stray cat. But this wasn't really different from her usual behavior, so he wasn't worried. She'd just have to get used to that sort of thing over time. The more she normalized being outside, the easier a time she'd have with it. They just had to be patient.

"Ready?"

"Okay."

They stepped away from their building and headed toward her junior high.

It was a typical Sunday morning. Still early, only nine AM. And with winter fast approaching, the air was quite chilly. In the shade, it felt like your body temperature was in free fall.

As cold as the air felt, the neighborhood seemed cozy and relaxed. Full lazy Sunday style. The lack of people rushing to work or school made even familiar streets look different.

They took their time, walking slowly toward Kaede's school. It was still a ways off, still out of sight, but each step Kaede took brought her that much closer to it. And that shortening distance was palpable.

Kaede wasn't a fast walker to begin with, but she was making steady progress.

She did freeze up when a car passed them but had no real problems making it all the way to the first turn.

But there she hit a brick wall.

At the intersection, they ran into some female students, walking up from their right. Two of them, wearing the same uniform as Kaede. They had racket cases with them—a bit too small to be tennis. Probably members of the badminton team off to practice.

They both glanced at Kaede.

Their eyes met.

"!"

Kaede shot up straight. She went stiff as a board.

Neither girl seemed to notice. They walked right past Sakuta and Kaede and continued on toward school.

Happy chatter about what they'd seen on TV the night before hung in the air.

Their laughter seemed to frighten Kaede, and she hid behind Sakuta. She took a tight grip on his clothes, and he could feel her hands shaking.

"They're not laughing at you, Kaede."

"You're sure?"

"If you think it's that easy to make people laugh, you're sorely mistaken."

"Th-the path to comedy greatness is paved with thorns!"

Kaede poked her head out from behind him, looking after the pair of girls. They were pretty far off now. Kaede had stopped shaking but had definitely lost her nerve. She was almost crouching. It didn't look like she would be going any farther.

They were maybe one hundred yards away from home.

Another eight to nine hundred to school.

The goal seemed pretty far off.

But Sakuta figured that was enough practice for one day. He turned back, looking Kaede over. There was a faint bruise on the skin of her thighs, below the hem of her skirt. One that hadn't been there when they left.

"Good work today," he said. "Let's go home and have some pudding."

They'd actually gotten farther than he'd expected for the first day of practice. He'd figured she'd lock up right outside their building.

"I—I don't want to quit yet!" she said. But her hands clutching his shoulders had started shaking again. She was clearly forcing herself. And he felt like the bruise on her thigh was getting darker, driven by her fears.

"Then let's just do one more step," he said, wanting to respect her resolve.

"Okay!" Kaede said, a little nervous.

But despite what she said, Kaede didn't take another step.

They waited five minutes, then ten...but she didn't manage it that day.

2

The next morning was Monday, November 24. He woke up earlier than usual.

He'd set his alarm for six thirty. Painfully early for Sakuta.

It wasn't for his health or anything.

It was so he could help Kaede with her walk-to-school practice.

If they went at the usual commute time, the roads would be packed with students. They'd talked about it last night and decided to go in earlier, like she was headed to morning practice with a team or club.

Plus, if they practiced when they usually did on the weekends, Sakuta wouldn't make it to school in time. He didn't really have a problem skipping school for days on end, but Kaede objected to it, so they were getting up early.

"You have to go to school and study!" Kaede said. "You have to go to the same college as Mai!"

Sakuta totally agreed with her there. Who knew what punishment awaited him if he failed?

Their first morning practice started off well, like the day before. But only at first. Kaede's feet stopped at the exact same place as last time.

The first intersection from their apartment.

Once again, they'd run into some students in her uniform. This time, it was three boys with crew cuts. Definitely baseball team hairdos. All three of them had their phones out, playing some sort of puzzle game.

Somehow they were walking to school, playing the game, and talking about homework all at the same time.

Kaede watched them from behind a telephone pole.

Her knees had buckled, but she was still motivated.

"I—I can keep going!" she said before Sakuta could suggest turning back.

Her voice quivered, and she looked pretty pale. She was obviously forcing herself. There was a bruise rising up her calf from her socks. A nasty, dark one, like a snake coiling around her leg.

It was hard to look at that and say, "Sure, let's keep going." Whatever Kaede herself might want, it was Sakuta's job to stop her from going too far.

"I've got to go to school, though," he said. "Should we call it a day?"

"O-okay. I don't want to make you late."

The same thing happened the next day.

Wednesday, November 26.

Kaede was acting strange all morning. Even when they first woke up, she seemed lost in thought, slow to react when Sakuta spoke to her.

He made the scrambled eggs that were her current favorite, but she just ate them in silence. No cries of "So good! I feel like my cheeks will fall off!" What was going on?

"......"

She changed into her uniform and put her shoes on, more on edge than usual.

"Kaede?" he said as they rode the elevator down.

She didn't answer.

"Earth to Kaede."

"Y-yes? What is it?"

"Is something the matter?"

"I've made up my mind. I'm going all the way to school today!"

She was suddenly all smiles. It didn't really answer his question, but their conversations were often a bit disjointed. That in itself wasn't too unusual. Just…this time there were a lot of factors in play, and they were all tangled together, so it was hard to take it as her usual ditzy charm.

"I'm ready to go!" she announced.

But Sakuta sensed some tension behind that smile. Almost panic.

"No need to rush it."

"I-I'm not rushing it!"

She forced a smile and denied it, but he could tell that wasn't really a smile. When their eyes met, she fled his gaze and hung her head.

"…I'm going to school," she whispered. Her hands clutching her skirt tight. Like she was barely holding on.

"Ms. Tomobe said to take your time."

"……" She said something, but he couldn't make it out.

"Kaede?"

"…That's not good enough."

This time, he could just barely hear it. Her voice shook. But there was a strength beneath that, a clarity of purpose. But that felt wrong to him. Made him worry.

"It isn't?"

"……"

No response.

The elevator doors opened before either said another word. The ding broke the silence.

Sakuta didn't step off.

He felt like they should probably not practice today. There was no need to try if it was gonna make her look like this. Forcing it was verboten. Miwako had said as much. Making herself try would just reinforce the idea that going to school was *hard*, and that was exactly what they didn't want. If she got it in her head that she couldn't do this, it would be a long time before she would be ready to try again.

That was what Miwako had told him.

It made sense. If you summoned all your courage and tried real hard and it ended in failure, how could you bring yourself to try again? Giving up was so much easier.

"Kaede, let's not today."

He pressed the button to close the doors. But as he did, someone raced past him. Kaede had jumped out of the elevator.

"Kaede!"

Sakuta threw himself bodily between the doors as they closed, calling after her.

But Kaede didn't turn back. She made a beeline toward the front entrance, but she wasn't exactly steady on her feet. She almost tripped and fell, but she threw her hands out onto the tiles and picked herself up. Without a glance back at him, she stepped outside the building.

"Kaede!" he yelled again, hurrying after her. "Wait up, Kaede!"

He was getting real loud, completely forgetting how early in the morning it was. His voice echoed across the street.

But Kaede just kept going. Running down the road to school, legs flying everywhere. She was not at all fast. Sakuta caught up with her easily.

He grabbed her wrist.

"You don't have to force yourself," he said.

"I do!" she exploded, already out of breath. "I don't have time to take my time!"

Her head snapped up, and she looked him right in the eye. Gaze not wavering at all. A teary-eyed glare.

He'd never seen her look like this.

And never heard her voice this ragged.

But that wasn't what surprised him the most. It was her words.

Kaede *knew*. She understood the situation she was in. She was fully aware she was running out of time.

And once Sakuta realized that, the strength drained out of his hand. He let go of Kaede's wrist.

Kaede turned to run away again. No—she was running toward school.

"So she knew this whole time," he muttered, watching her stagger off.

Her words and actions both made that clear.

The realization shook him to his core. His head was spinning, trying to work out what to do. Lost in thought, his body froze up. No instructions were being relayed by his brain.

But that lasted only for a moment.

He peeled his feet off the pavement. Once he took that first step, the rest was easy. Body and soul went chasing after Kaede.

And as he did, his thoughts caught up with him—or rather, he decided that thinking about it was pointless.

Ahead of him, Kaede had come to an abrupt stop. The same intersection she always got stuck at. A girl in uniform had crossed the street in front of her.

Their eyes must have met.

Kaede hung her head, moving to the edge of the path, hiding behind a telephone pole. She crouched down, still out of breath from all the running. Her shoulders heaving.

But a moment later, she forced herself back to her feet, like she was wringing out every bit of strength she had. Even after rising to her feet, her body refused to take another step forward.

"Why... Why...?"

As he got closer, he could hear her whispering, her voice shaking.

"Why can't I do it?"

She was punching her thighs, pounding away at them.

Sakuta caught up and grabbed her arms, stopping that. There were huge bruises on her thighs where she'd been hitting herself. And purple specks on her arms, as well. These weren't from the force of her blows, but from her Adolescence Syndrome. It hurt to look at.

"Why… Why…? I want to go to school! Why can't I?"

There were huge tears rolling down her face. She was staring down at her legs, as if rebuking her own body.

"Why, why, why?!"

What was this even directed at now? Herself? The other person inside her? Or maybe both.

"Kaede," he said.

She wouldn't look at him.

"I'm not going back," she said, her voice a sob.

She threw her arms around the telephone pole.

"I'm not," she said again, like a stubborn child. "I'm practicing until I make it to school."

Her face was a mess of tears and snot.

"I have to practice…!"

"I know."

He made his voice sound like it always did. This wasn't an answer he'd prepared. It was one he'd found while watching her suffer like this. He didn't know if it was the right decision. He couldn't be sure, but rather than waste time worrying about the answer, he chose to spend all his time following through.

"I know," he said again.

Kaede's shoulders twitched.

"I'll make sure you can go to school."

"You will?" Kaede said, finally looking at him again. He could see his face reflected in her tears. "Really?"

"I swear."

"You really swear?"

"I do."

She didn't seem to believe him yet. Her mouth was hanging open.

"But I think we need to rest a bit before we try again."

He rummaged around in his pockets and pulled out some tissues he'd been handed at the station ages back. He used those to clean up Kaede's face.

"Rest?" she said. A little late.

"Yeah. I know a great place to rest. Lemme show you."

He turned around and started walking away.

"Oh! Wait for me!" Kaede said. She let go of the telephone pole and hurried after him. Soon she was attached to his shoulder.

3

They went back home and washed Kaede's face properly, and then Sakuta called Minegahara High.

"This is Sakuta Azusagawa from Class 2-1. I'm not feeling good, so I'm gonna take the day off," he lied and then hung up.

He waited a bit, but it didn't seem like they planned to call back, so he and Kaede left again at around nine thirty.

Kaede took a step toward school, but he stopped her.

"This way," he said, beckoning.

Then he led her to Fujisawa Station.

This was a huge building with three lines running through it. They were past the peak of rush hour, but it was still packed. Half the crowd was going in the gates and half pouring out.

"There's so many people!" Kaede said, hiding behind him.

She'd stopped in her tracks, but if they couldn't get past this, they'd never reach their destination.

"If you get stuck here, you'll never make it to school, Kaede."

"R-right! I can do it!"

Kaede regained some of her spirit and raised her head. They bought tickets at the JR machines and went through the gates.

A train pulled into the platform, silver with orange and green stripes. This was the Tokaido Line.

Sakuta and Kaede boarded a Koganei-bound car.

There were empty seats in the back, so he put Kaede by the window and sat down next to her.

"A-are we still not at this 'great place'?" Kaede asked as the train pulled out. She was very conscious of the crowd around her.

"Don't worry, we'll be there soon."

The train soon stopped at the next station. Ofuna Station, one stop down the line. Some people got off; some got on.

The bell rang, the doors closed, and the train pulled out again.

"Still not there?"

"A bit farther."

The next stop was Totsuka. Sakuta and Kaede did not get off.

"*Still* not there?"

"Just a bit more."

Then it stopped at Yokohama Station. Once again, Sakuta and Kaede stayed on the train. They'd been riding it for a good twenty minutes now.

"How much farther?"

"Hmm, not that much longer."

They repeated this at every station. After Yokohama, it stopped at Kawasaki, Shinagawa, Shinbashi, and Tokyo. Even when it pulled out of Tokyo Station, Sakuta and Kaede were still on board.

"You're lying to me!" Kaede said. She was getting increasingly upset.

"I swear, this time we're almost there."

"Y-you can't fool me!"

She puffed out her cheeks angrily.

But this time he really meant it. They were getting off at the next station.

"See? We're here."

He could see the platform through the windows. The train slowed to a stop, right where it should.

The doors opened.

Sakuta and Kaede stepped out.

There was a sign right in front of them with the station name.

Ueno

Sakuta and Kaede had disembarked at a large station in Tokyo's Taito Ward, a building where old and new were all jumbled together. It lay on the east side of Tokyo, surrounded by universities, art galleries, and museums. It was a short walk to Asakusa, home of the famous Kaminarimon. It was a clear day, and you could easily make out the Skytree in the distance.

But they weren't here for any of that.

Outside the platform gates, Sakuta followed the signs that read PARK EXIT. This took them out the north side of the station. The park the exit was named after spread out in front of them.

They headed inside.

"Wh-where exactly are we going?" Kaede asked. All of this was extremely uncharted territory for her. She hadn't let go of his arm since they boarded the train.

"Somewhere great," he said evasively.

He led them between the Bunka Kaikan and the National Museum of Western Art.

Their destination came into view. The front gates up ahead.

"Sakuta?" Kaede said, still lost.

It was a weekday morning. Not even eleven AM. Yet even at this hour, there was a mass of people wandering around. Lots of groups of women out for a stroll and catching up on gossip. Kaede seemed too preoccupied by the crowds to notice their destination.

"Look up," he said.

She blinked, glancing up at him. Then she followed his gaze, turning to face front.

"Oh!" she said. "The zoo?"

Surprised, she read the words on the gate.

"The zoo!" she said again, this time really excited.

Sakuta had taken Kaede to the zoo in Ueno. Supposedly the first zoo opened in Japan.

"We're at the zoo, Sakuta!" she said, tugging his sleeve.

"I said it would be great, didn't I?"

He bought two tickets, and they went inside.

They felt the change in the air immediately.

"It smells like Nasuno when she needs a bath!" Kaede said, eyes sparkling.

"Yep, sure does."

At the moment, all they could see were people, though. College couples, mysterious old men here alone, groups of kids with backpacks. Sakuta and Kaede were in uniform, but there were enough schools on field trips that they didn't really stand out. The lady at the ticket gate had given them a dubious look but hadn't cared enough to actually probe.

A few steps inside the gates, Kaede suddenly stopped. "Oh," she said.

"What?" he asked, thinking something had happened.

"Pandas!" she said, beaming back at him.

The panda exhibit lay directly ahead, with a huge sign advertising it.

"Sakuta, pandas! They have pandas!" she said, pulling his arm. "Come on!" she said.

Straight to the panda exhibit. Totally unconcerned about anyone around them. There was clearly nothing left in her brain except seeing the pandas as soon as possible.

He'd never seen Kaede like this.

That alone made him think it was worth bringing her here.

She pulled him into the building housing the exhibit. There was a crowd gathered at the back. Two pandas in an outdoor enclosure. Their distinctive black-and-white fur.

"Pandas! Real-life pandas!"

A group had just moved on, so a front row spot opened up for them.

Kaede leaned over the railing.

A panda was walking by so close you could almost touch it.

"A panda! Walking!"

"It is walking, yes."

Seeing them up close like this was impressive. They were pretty big.

"That panda's eating!"

The other panda was at the back of the enclosure, munching on some bamboo. Its legs sprawled out in front of it, kicking back.

"It's eating all right."

It sure was chowing down. Didn't seem to have any interest in the two of them. Just doing what it did.

"Pandas are so big!"

"Well, they are 'giant.'"

"And black and white!"

"So are zebras."

"Ah! It just looked at me!"

Kaede waved. The panda didn't bat an eye. It just kept eating.

"Damn, it's still eating."

"Bamboo isn't very nutritious, so it has to spend most of the day eating just to stay alive. I saw that on TV."

"Being a panda sounds hard."

"Everyone has their own challenges."

Even as they talked, Kaede's eyes never left the pandas. She

watched them for nearly an hour without showing any signs of boredom or fatigue.

"The pandas have been eating this whole time!"

Both of them were eating now. One of them hadn't done anything else the entire time they'd been standing here.

The TV had clearly been right about pandas.

But at that moment, Sakuta's stomach growled.

"I think I'm hungry, too," Kaede said, putting a hand on her belly.

It was almost noon. In a place like this, it was probably better to eat before the crowds arrived.

"Then let's grab a bite somewhere."

Outside the panda exhibit, they followed the guide posts, looking for a place to eat. They found themselves in a cafeteria. It was already pretty packed.

He was a little worried that Kaede wouldn't hold out long enough to get food, but his concerns proved unfounded.

She usually got nervous in places like this, but today she just accompanied him like any other person he knew. The lingering excitement from the pandas seemed to have left her too giddy to notice the people around her.

Kaede decided to order the Panda Udon. This dish made a panda face out of grated yam and shiitake mushrooms. It came with a piece of seaweed that had a panda drawn on it. Clearly, the pandas were the stars of the park. If they made Kaede this happy, he wanted one at home.

Once they finished eating, they strolled around the rest of the park. There were plenty of other animals. Elephants and bears, lions and tigers, a ton of birds. Even some gorillas. They checked out the sea lions, the seals, the polar bears, and the capybaras, then took the monorail to the west side of the zoo.

There they enjoyed the pygmy hippos and okapi. Along with the pandas, the zoo called these three of the most famous endangered species. They were all pretty fascinating creatures.

"I definitely like the pandas best," Kaede said. She'd seemed lost in thought, but apparently she'd just been battling the lure of the okapi.

Once they finished making the rounds of the west side, they crossed the bridge back to the east. On the way, they found the red pandas.

"Sakuta, red pandas!"

"They're definitely red."

"And so small!"

"They're also called lesser pandas."

"But cute!"

They watched the red pandas for a long time.

Then they heard another girl's voice say, "Look! Red pandas!"

They looked back and saw a petite girl, early teens, clinging to a man's arm—probably her brother.

"They do seem 'lesser.'"

"How so?"

"They aren't 'giant.'"

"Huh."

He appeared to be blowing off his sister's chatter. He didn't seem like a college student—more like he was in his midtwenties. Probably had a job and everything. He kept turning his head, like he was looking for someone.

"Where'd she go?"

"She still not picking up?" his sister asked.

The man pulled out his phone and tried again.

"No luck," he said, looking defeated.

"Can't believe a grown-up would get herself lost like this." For some reason, the sister smiled like this was a major victory.

"And whose fault is that?"

"You're supposed to be looking after her, so this is clearly your fault."

"You're the one who suddenly stopped following that grade school class around!"

"Well, the teacher started waving at me."

"You're in your twenties, and she really thought you were in her class…"

Sakuta almost made a noise. He'd figured the sister was in junior high, but apparently she was a fully grown adult. Older than him even. But she looked Kaede's age or younger. The world had all kinds of little sisters in it.

"We're gonna have to have them call for her over the loudspeakers, aren't we?"

"I dunno if they'll even do that for a grown-up…"

But even as the spoke, the loudspeaker crackled to life.

"W-we have a lost…grown-up. She's five foot three, long hair, midtwenties, carrying a sketchbook. If you know her, come to the West Monorail Station, please."

The woman making the announcement was clearly a bit flummoxed by the whole situation, and the visitors nearby were all going, "A lost grown-up?" But they all soon decided it didn't matter and went back to touring the zoo.

"They're calling for you," the sister said.

"…Yeah, they are."

Looking suddenly tired, the siblings left the red panda exhibit and headed toward the monorail station.

Once the mystery siblings were gone, Sakuta and Kaede said good-bye to the red pandas and continued east.

They wandered the gardens awhile and found themselves near the gift shop. It was jam-packed with animal merchandise. Including panda stuff. Lots of panda stuff. They ended up looking at the stuffed animals. There were two pandas at this zoo, so they sold two types of stuffed pandas.

"I—I could make do with only one, you know? It's just—they might get lonely if you don't buy both."

"Okay, okay."

Sakuta's wallet was definitely getting lighter. And the weight on his shoulders got that much heavier—because he soon had two stuffed pandas in his backpack

By the time they left the gift shop, the sun was setting. The sky to the west had turned red. It was almost closing time.

Sakuta and Kaede stopped by the panda exhibit one last time on the way to the exit.

"The pandas…are still eating."

It wasn't clear if they'd been eating the entire time Sakuta and Kaede were looking at other animals. But they were sitting in the exact same spot, legs splayed out. Did bamboo really taste that good?

The loudspeaker announced the park was closing, so they made their way to the exit.

Kaede was walking very slowly and kept turning back to look at the panda building. It was obvious she was reluctant to part ways.

"I'll miss those pandas."

"You can always come again."

"But I might not…" She trailed off, hanging her head.

Sakuta figured she meant she might not get a chance. And he couldn't very well promise she would. He didn't know what would happen.

So…instead, he said, "This one's yours," and handed her the ticket he'd bought on the way in. It wasn't an ordinary ticket.

"Oh…," Kaede said, realizing as much. She was reading the writing on the ticket closely. It clearly said *Annual Passport*, and it had *Kaede* (in hiragana) *Azusagawa* written in the name field above the green lines.

"With that, you can come see the pandas every day."

"W-wow! Y-you really are my brother!"

"Was that ever in question?"

"But, then…"

"Mm?"

"I *can* come here again. Right?"

She looked to him for confirmation, on the verge of tears. Thinking about the old Kaede, afraid she might not always be this Kaede.

Nobody could blame you for being yourself.

"Of course!" Sakuta said.

As long as it was new Kaede with him, he was going to be *her* brother. He wanted to make sure that she didn't feel afraid to be herself. So this could be normal for her, like it was for everyone else. He'd do anything he could to make that true.

"I mean, I paid for an annual pass; you'd better not waste it."

"If I come often enough, it pays for itself!"

"That's the spirit."

"I know!"

And Kaede passed through the exit with a smile on her face.

4

Kaede remained excited on the way home, even after they reached Fujisawa Station. The whole walk back, she couldn't stop talking about the pandas and the other animals and which ones she liked and which were the cutest.

They stopped at a convenience store between their apartment building and the station. Sakuta wasn't quite sure how this logical leap had occurred, but Kaede had insisted that if pandas' staple diet was bamboo, then hers was pudding, and they had to buy some.

Kaede spent a long time thinking about which pudding she wanted.

"I'll take these!" she said, putting two puddings in the basket.

Sakuta turned to take them to the register, but she stopped him.

"Oh, wait! Can I do it?"

He didn't see any reason why not, so he handed her the basket and a one-thousand-yen note.

"H-here I go!" she said.

Sakuta watched as she carried the basket to the front of the shop. The clerk behind the counter was a college-aged girl with her hair dyed brown.

"I-I'll take these!" Kaede said, looking nervous. She set the basket on the counter.

The clerk quickly scanned the bar codes and put the two puddings in a bag.

It was very clear that Kaede found this interaction stressful. She was fidgeting all over the place.

But she managed to hand over the bill and receive her change. She almost forgot to take the puddings, and the clerk had to call out and hand the bag to her.

"Th-thank you!" Kaede said, bobbing her head.

"Thank you," the clerk said with a smile.

This was apparently super embarrassing, so Kaede turned and hustled back to Sakuta.

"I—I went shopping!" she said.

"Almost forgot your pudding, though."

"Good thing she was nice."

The clerk must have heard them because she started laughing. What did she make of this whole business? At the very least, they weren't like her usual customers.

It wasn't an unpleasant laugh, though. More like she'd seen something adorable and couldn't help but smile.

Kaede handed him the change as they left.

"Should I carry the pudding?" he asked, holding out his hand.

Kaede twisted herself, hiding the pudding behind her.

"I bought the pudding, so I'll carry it."

She was in a *very* good mood. She kept peering into the bag and grinning.

Successfully buying something must have been a real thrill.

Not far from the store was a bridge that spanned the Sakai River. If you followed this river downstream, it came out close to Enoshima.

They usually hung a left after the bridge, but instead Sakuta kept going straight.

"Sakuta, we live that way." Kaede pointed.

"I know a shortcut," he said, lying through his teeth. He didn't stop.

"I had no idea there was a shortcut this way!" Kaede didn't suspect a thing.

"You have a lot to learn about our neighborhood."

"But you know everything?"

"I'm an expert."

"That's amazing."

The farther they walked, the more houses there were. The quiet of the night increased the farther they got from the station. But you could still hear cars passing in the distance, and there were lights shining in the apartment complexes, so it was never all that dark.

After a five-minute walk, they turned a corner and found themselves by a large gate.

"Huh?" Kaede said, surprised. "S-Sakuta! Is that…?"

There was an athletic field visible beyond the gate. A soccer goal gleamed white in the glow of the streetlights. And past that field was a three-story building.

Sakuta had led Kaede to her junior high school. The same place she'd been desperately trying to reach all week.

The lights were out, and it was shrouded in the silence of night. Like the school itself was asleep.

"S-school!"

"It's pretty late, so let's keep it down."

"Gasp!" Kaede clapped her hand over her mouth.

He gave her a sidelong glance, then reached for the gate. He gave it a good tug, but it didn't budge. It wasn't very tall, though, so it could easily be scaled.

"Hokay," he grunted as he landed inside.

"W-we can't!"

"C'mon," he said, holding out his hand.

"N-no way!"

"Just a peek."

"...Just..."

"Just what?"

"Just for a minute."

She'd definitely had to think about it for a second, but in the end, she took his hand. Her desire to go inside won out over the idea that this was against the rules. Sakuta helped her scramble over the fence.

Kaede landed inside the schoolyard on both feet, keeping her puddings safe.

"......"

"Your first day at school."

"My first *night* at school."

"Man, *night school* kinda sounds dirty," he joked and started walking toward the school building.

Kaede followed, craning her head in all directions.

It looked like the third-year classes were on the first floor, overlooking the athletic field. Peering at the wall by the blackboard, he couldn't make out which class it was but saw *third-year* written clearly. Evidently, this school made the younger kids do all the climbing.

"Oh, this is Class 3-1," he said, finally finding a sign at the back.

"This is my classroom?"

More than thirty desks and chairs. A blackboard covered in chalk dust. A podium placed at an angle. Kaede put her hands up against the glass, peering at all of it. Naturally, there was no one in the darkened space.

A minute or two...maybe longer. She stood in silence, staring into the room.

"Sakuta," she said softly.

"Mm?"

"I'd like to come here during the day next."

"Now that you've conquered night school, you'll have no problems."

"Y-you think?"

"I mean, ghosts come out at night. Way more frightening."

"G-ghosts?!" Kaede let out a little shriek.

"Mm? Did I just see something move?" he said while exaggeratedly glancing through the windows. This was a chance to wind her up a bit, after all.

"What?! Oh no, there is something long and white!" Kaede yelped, pointing.

"Yeah, it's a curtain."

"I-it might be a ghost! I've learned my lesson. No more night school! W-we should get going."

She started pulling his arm.

"Yeah, probably time."

He let her drag him across the center of the field.

Back at the front gate, they clambered over it once more.

Kaede stayed attached to Sakuta for a bit, but she finally let go once they could see their apartment building.

"Sakuta."

"What?"

"I can put circles next to everything in my notebook now!"

"Oh, already? Wow."

"Pandas, pudding, and school make it complete!"

"Well, we should celebrate."

"Yes! But I think I'm going to mark the school with a triangle."

"I think a circle would be just fine."

Kaede shook her head.

"Only when I've made it there in daylight."

"Okay."

"But I feel like I can do it."

"Mm?"

"I think tomorrow I'll be able to go to school in daylight!"

Sakuta wasn't sure what the basis for that was coming from. But…

"Yeah," he said. It seemed like the natural answer.

"I can't wait for tomorrow!"

Kaede smiled with the utmost confidence, and Sakuta found himself believing in her.

"Tomorrow's gonna be great!" Kaede said, her smile gleaming under the night sky.

Tomorrow *would* be a good day.

That was what her smile told him.

5

Something was tickling his mouth.

Like someone was stroking him with a soft brush.

No sooner was he aware of this than something licked the bridge of his nose.

"Meow."

A grumpy-sounding cry penetrated his slumber. That was Nasuno.

Sakuta half opened his eyes, staring blearily up at their tricolored cat.

"You hungry?"

"Mrow."

Nasuno was standing on his chest.

"What time is it?"

Fighting off the urge to go back to bed, he reached for the clock.

It showed half past seven. Morning already. His mind started to clear. His eyes snapped open.

The sunlight through the curtains insisted it was morning.

Sakuta moved to get up, and Nasuno hastily jumped down onto his bed. Sakuta sat up a moment later.

Usually, Kaede was here to wake him up by now, but there was no sign of her. Nor was she burrowed under his covers. It was weirdly quiet outside.

"Maybe she's trapped in bed with muscle pain again?"

They had run all around the zoo yesterday. That might have taken its toll on her. He recalled how their trip to the beach a few weeks ago had put her completely out of commission.

Remembering how feeble she'd been, Sakuta left his room.

He washed his face and got breakfast ready. He was running late, so it was just toast, yogurt, and sliced tomato with eggs sunny-side up.

He put two plates of this on the dining room table.

No sounds emerged from Kaede's room this whole time.

"Kaede, breakfast's ready. Can you get up?" he called through the door.

"……"

No answer.

He had no choice. "Coming in," he said as he opened the door before stepping into Kaede's room.

"*Zzz… Zzz…*"

She was sound asleep. Blissfully slumbering.

In her usual panda pajamas.

On either side of her were the stuffed pandas they'd bought at the zoo. It almost looked like a panda and her cubs. That thought made Sakuta laugh out loud.

"Kaede, it's morning. You gonna sleep all day?"

"Mm?" she grumbled.

Her brow furrowed. An unhappy, sleepy look.

But the expression soon relaxed. "Mm," she groaned again, and her eyes fluttered open.

She sat up. No muscle pain, then. She sat with her legs stretched out for a full five seconds, then said, "Mornin'."

She rubbed her eyes and looked up at him.

She seemed really out of it.

"……"

Something about this response seemed off. Had Kaede *ever* said "Mornin'" like that? She normally said "Good morning!" instead.

As that thought echoed through his mind, he started noticing more irregularities.

Something was wrong. Different.

A silent alarm whistle started blowing inside his head. Getting louder. And as it did, a frown appeared on her face.

"Uh…?" she said, blinking. "You are Sakuta, right?"

Why would she ask *that*?

"…Yeah," he said. Why was he responding like this?

The doubt growing in his mind suddenly erupted, and his heart skipped a beat. Then two, then three, his pulse racing.

"You grew your hair out?"

Kaede was right in front of him but seemed so far away.

"That doesn't happen overnight," he said.

He could hear his own voice, but it felt like someone else was talking.

"Huh? But…," she whined. Like this didn't make sense. It was a slightly spoiled response.

Sakuta already had his answer. He just couldn't find the words.

"Uh, Kaede…"

"What?"

"Do you…?" The rest got stuck in his throat.

"Spit it out already," she said, trying to get up. "Ugh, my legs are killing me."

"You ran around the zoo a lot yesterday."

"The zoo?" She blinked at him. "We didn't go to the zoo. What's wrong with you?"

She peered up at him, looking worried.

"Uh, we did, though…"

"We did *not*. I mean, yesterday… Uh, what did we do yesterday?"

She stopped, thinking. Nothing came to mind, a fact that seemed to surprise her.

"So you don't remember, then." His voice was a dry croak.

"……?" Kaede tilted her head, totally lost.

"You were all happy about the pandas. We bought those stuffed animals."

They were lying on the bed. Kaede picked one up.

"Oh, these are cute. What about 'em, though?" she asked.

"……"

There was no need to keep digging.

"Uh, wait, what's with this room? Was my room like this?"

This wasn't just "off." This was completely different. It wasn't Kaede.

He couldn't stop himself from asking.

"You're…Kaede, then?" He meant his old sister.

"Who else would I be? What's gotten into you?"

That faint smile, like she was being tickled. A smile he hadn't seen since they lost the old Kaede.

His racing heartbeat soon settled down.

He wasn't surprised or flustered. This was happening very fast, but he managed to avoid melting down in front of her.

But his whole body felt weird. Like there was a mist over his eyes. Like everything was really far away.

That was the only difference. His head itself was clear. "Hang on a minute," he said.

He left Kaede's room and called his dad.

"What's the matter, Sakuta?" his father answered.

"Kaede's got her memories back."

There was a long silence. "You're sure?" he asked at last.

"Pretty sure. I don't think I'd fail to recognize her."

"Yeah."

"I'm gonna take her to the hospital. Can you come?"

"Got it. Same one?"

"Mm-hmm."

"Then I'll see you there. Take care of her for me?"

"Got it."

The whole call was very calm.

Neither of them got emotional at all.

They hung up, and Sakuta picked up the receiver again. He needed to let the hospital know they were on their way.

He explained her condition and that he'd like them to take a look. They said they'd be ready.

Then he made one last call. To a taxi dispatcher.

When they got to the hospital, the same psychiatrist and neurologist were waiting for them.

After the initial exams, they said she'd need to stay for a few days so they could run some more detailed tests.

Sakuta had expected that.

"Okay," he said, nodding.

Sitting next to him, Kaede still didn't seem to have a real handle on her situation. She had a look of perpetual surprise on her face.

She seemed like she didn't know why she was in the hospital or why they were running all these tests.

When their father arrived, the doctor explained, "It appears that she doesn't remember anything that happened while she had amnesia. At the moment, she doesn't seem to really be conscious of that, but I believe in time the missing memories will cause her some consternation. Perhaps it would be best to keep her here until that settles down."

Their father bowed his head. "Please do," he said. Sakuta followed suit mechanically. Everything still seemed to be removed from himself. None of it felt real.

Once the initial examination and a few basic tests were done, Kaede was led to her room to wait.

When Sakuta and their father finished talking to the doctors and caught up with her, she looked anxious. She still didn't get why she was here.

"I mean, there's nothing wrong with me," she said with a kinda bratty sulk.

"She really is Kaede." There was a quiver in their father's voice. It had been two years since he'd seen his daughter.

He'd been forced to bottle up his love for her, and now it was all raging through him. He'd spent two years waiting for this day to arrive, trusting that it would…and now it finally had.

"D-Dad? What's wrong?"

Sakuta looked up, and there were tears in his father's eyes.

"No, these are just…" But there was no denying this.

His shoulders shook. He was crying tears of joy.

"Wh-what's even going on? This is so awkward…," Kaede said.

"Yeah," their dad said. He tried to choke it back but failed.

"Argh," Kaede said, looking even more lost.

Two years since his father had seen his daughter, but Sakuta just stood there watching. It all still felt like all this was happening in some far-off place. Like it wasn't real. Like he was watching an old movie.

Kaede had her memories back, but he couldn't rejoice in that fact the way his dad was. He saw the reasons to be overjoyed, and he knew it was a happy event, but the expected emotions never surfaced. They wouldn't come out. They were clinging to something massive lurking inside him. Something that pulled them in and swallowed them.

And whatever that massive thing was, it was getting bigger as time went on. Threatening to spill out of him.

And once he became aware of that, he felt a heat building up behind his eyes. A prickling sensation at the back of his nose. A sob almost escaped his throat. Something inside was screaming at him to hurry. Yelling for him to get the hell out of here.

"Gonna hit the bathroom." After a curt remark, he was in the hall before either his father or Kaede could respond.

And he was off down the corridor before the door closed. His pace got faster and faster, and halfway down the hall, he was at a full run. By the time he left the hospital, he was going as fast as he could.

A nurse tried to yell at him, but he couldn't hear her.

He'd been happy to have the old Kaede back at first. He'd felt it when he saw how happy his father was. But those feelings were pushed aside and swept away by the huge wave that came up after them.

Letting this new wave crest in the hospital room, in front of Kaede and his father? He'd been pretty sure that would not end well.

His emotions had finally caught up to what was happening. And the sense of loss was swallowing up everything else. It was a monster, maw gaping wide, consuming everything in its path.

There was no escaping it. It was inside him. But he ran anyway. That was all he could do.

Soon the darkness caught him.

"Augh…"

As he left the hospital grounds, Sakuta clutched his chest, crouching down.

"Aughhhhhhh…!"

He couldn't put these emotions into words. He couldn't, but if he didn't get them out, somehow it felt like his head would explode.

All he could see was the ground and his own feet. He was desperately trying to hold back the tears, but big drops were already falling all around him. Only then did he notice it was raining really hard.

"We said we'd go see the pandas again!" He yelled so loud it felt like his throat nearly tore open. "You said you'd go so many times that the pass would pay for itself!"

He was venting everything raging within.

"You said you thought you'd finally make it to school tomorrow. You said…you would…"

The words were crumbling. His voice cracked. His heart was shattering.

"That's what you said, Kaede!"

The rain slammed against his back, but he couldn't feel it. He could only feel one thing. A single, searing pain.

"Owww…"

His hand clutched his chest.

It hurt. Hurt beyond all measure.

He looked down, and something red was seeping through his T-shirt.

"……"

His fingers were turning red now.

His plain T-shirt had been stained red from the inside.

"…God damn it," he muttered.

Such a simple thing to say in the face of this inexplicable event. No pain or surprise.

"God damn it," he said again.

The red stain steadily spread.

He didn't know why the hell this was happening, but he'd seen this happen before. It was the Adolescence Syndrome that had beset him two years earlier.

He knew logically that this was that same thing happening again. And that was exactly why his response was just pure irritation. All it did was piss him off.

Why now? Of all the moments to come back, why get in his way now?

"God damn it…"

This should have elicited stronger emotion, but it came out limp. His body just couldn't keep up. Emotions with no outlet flailed uselessly.

All he could do was crouch there, unable to stand, like he'd forgotten how to move.

"What the hell…why this?! Why now?!"

These questions were without a doubt directed at himself, at his own shortcomings.

Berating himself made his chest hurt even more. It hurt and it hurt and it hurt until he couldn't tell left from right. He couldn't even raise his head. All he could do was watch raindrops splatter against the pavement.

Then a pair of shoes entered his field of view. Small feet. Not a man's—this was a girl.

"You're okay."

Sakuta's mind was fading out, but he caught her voice.

"You're okay."

He heard it again. He wasn't imagining it.

He moved as if controlled by that voice, lifting his head. He felt like he *had* to. The girl's voice had that kind of power.

Heedless of the wet ground, she sat down next to Sakuta. Her hand on his shoulders, peering into his face.

"You're okay, Sakuta."

He knew her face.

"……"

He couldn't think anymore. He had no idea what was going on. Only one thing rose out of the chaos in his mind.

Her name.

It had been so, so long. But her name still mattered to him.

And like a child who's just learned to read, he said her name out loud.

"Shouko."

She smiled at him.

"Yes. It's me. I'm here now, and you're going to be okay."

6

He could hear the sound of rain.

Falling somewhere far away.

No, it only felt far away because he was inside and the window were closed.

He knew this room. Of course he did. Sakuta was in his own room.

Sitting on the side of the bed he always slept in.

The curtains were open. The rain outside was coming down hard. The sound of it just underscored how quiet it was inside.

It was like his room had been cut off from the rest of the world. All the sounds seemed far away.

With that thought, it finally dawned on Sakuta that he was home.

"Why am I…?"

His question was interrupted by a knock.

Even with the rain outside, this noise came loud and clear.

"Have you changed yet?"

The knock was followed by a gentle voice. There was a familiar warmth to it. Just hearing this voice made him want to cry.

But no tears came. His tear ducts did not respond at all.

"You're not answering, so I'm coming in. If you're half-changed, this is your own fault."

The door opened a crack, and Shouko poked her head in.

"Why, you haven't changed at all," she said, opening the door all the way.

Seeing her, Sakuta finally remembered how he'd gotten here. Shouko had shown up out of nowhere and taken him home.

She'd removed his soaked shoes and socks, then pushed him into his room, ordering him to change out of the rest of his wet things.

But the moment he was alone in his room, he'd ceased to care about anything. He'd slumped down on the edge of his bed, unable to summon the energy to move at all.

"You'll catch a cold!"

She wrapped a towel around his head and used it to dry his hair—being a bit rough with him.

"Okay, arms up."

He did as he was told. She pulled his long-sleeved T-shirt off. A bolt of pain shot through his chest. The shirt she just tore away had been stuck to the dried blood on his chest.

Three claw marks on his chest.

They looked like discolored welts, still healed over. Though now stained with dried blood. As was the long-sleeved T-shirt. It was soaked through with his blood.

He had so many questions. If his wounds hadn't opened, why had that much blood appeared? Enough to dye his clothes red? Why had the mysterious hemorrhage stopped? If the pain had been real, why was he okay now?

And most of all, he had questions about Shouko.

The Shouko rummaging around in his closet wasn't the first-year junior high Shouko Makinohara he'd met this summer.

This was the Shouko he'd met on the beach at Shichirigahama

two years ago. And as far as he could tell, she had grown two years older in the meantime.

Everything about this situation was a mystery. Enigmatic. Baffling.

But even as questions swirled around him, Sakuta felt like he didn't want to know the answers.

He didn't even care about that.

The only thing he cared about was the Kaede he'd lost.

That loss was so overwhelming it just made everything else seem unimportant.

Events around him seemed distant and hazy. Like there was a mist over everything.

Beyond that mist, Shouko turned toward him, having fished out a change of clothes from his closet. A new long-sleeved T-shirt and the pants from the tracksuit he wore around the house. Even a pair of underwear.

"I think the bath is almost ready. You'd better get in."

Shouko came over to him.

When he looked up, she grabbed his arms and pulled forcibly, trying to yank him to his feet.

He didn't see the point in fighting her, so he let her win.

Shouko maneuvered around behind him and pushed him into the changing room.

"Do you need me to take your pants and underwear off, too?" That almost sounded like a serious question.

"I can manage."

He couldn't be bothered to think.

His socks and shirt were already gone, so he dropped the rest of his clothes on the floor. Shouko was still here, and she said something, but he paid her no attention.

Moving away from her little shriek, he stepped into the bathroom and closed the door.

"G-geez, nobody asked to see that! I-I'll put your fresh clothes here."

Shouko was fuming away on the other side of the cloudy glass door. What was she so worked up about?

He scooped some water out of the bath and poured it over his head. His chest wounds were definitely healed. They didn't sting at all.

Once in the bathwater, it felt like some sensations returned to his body.

He stared at the ceiling for a while.

Then he said "Shouko" without consciously deciding to do so.

He could tell she was still in the changing room.

"Yes?" she asked.

"I...couldn't do anything."

No emotion in his voice.

"That's not true."

"But Kaede's..."

He was just stating the truth.

"You did great, Sakuta."

"What do you know, Shouko?"

The words were just sounds. There was no feeling or force behind them. They came out flat, the total opposite of the warmth in Shouko's tone. It didn't feel like his voice. But it was definitely Sakuta talking.

"I know you feel regret because you think there might have been more you could have done for Kaede."

"......"

"I know *everything*," she said.

She'd said things like that a lot. He remembered that about her and thought it was funny, but he didn't laugh. He wasn't in the mood. The gaping hole inside him was still swallowing all of that up. There was nothing left inside but an arid wind. The hollow sound it made echoed within him.

"Did Kaede ever act like you'd done something wrong?"

"……"

"She only ever acted like she adored you, Sakuta."

Shouko's voice was so warm. You could hear her heart in it.

"…Maybe I could have done more."

Before he knew it, the pain inside him was spilling out. He spat out the words like he was casting a curse on himself.

"You'll have to do that the next chance you get."

"But Kaede doesn't have another chance."

"If you keep this up, I'll feel sorry for her."

"……"

"She did everything she could to make sure you wouldn't be left with all these regrets."

"……"

He couldn't process what she meant. What did she even mean by *next chance*?

"Kaede was trying to make sure you knew that she was happy being with you."

"……"

"I feel sorry for Kaede if those feelings didn't reach you."

Shouko's outline in the clouded glass grew more distinct.

Then it shrank to half the height.

She'd sat down outside the bathroom door.

He could see something in her silhouette's hand. It was square. Shouko opened it like a book.

"'I'm starting a diary today. Kaede's diary. Sakuta gave me a new name, all hiragana. He bought me this notebook, too.'"

Shouko was clearly reading something aloud.

Sakuta knew exactly what it was. The notebook he'd given Kaede. That thick volume she'd used as a diary, stuffing it full of her thoughts.

But he had no idea what she'd written in there.

Shouko began to quietly read the rest.

*   *   *

I have a father, a mother, and a brother.
But I don't know them.
I'm told I have no memories.
The doctor said it was amnesia caused by a "dissociative disorder."
I don't know what that means.

I'm told I was someone else before.
A different Kaede. Old Kaede.
But I don't know that Kaede.
I've never met her.
This is so hard.

Today Mom and the doctor have been talking a lot.
Talking about my illness.
Am I sick?
I don't have a fever.
I'm not coughing.
My nose isn't running.
I feel fine.
But Mom keeps asking the doctor when I'll be better.
And that hurts.

What will happen to me if the other Kaede's memories come back?
Will I become her?
Where will I go?
Thinking about it is scary and makes me want to cry.

Mom and Dad seem really unhappy.
They always pat my head and say, "Take your time."
But I don't get it.
I'm me. I'm not her.
I got sad and cried a lot.

*   *   *

I said something really mean.

I told Mom and Dad I didn't want to be with them.

I'm sorry.

But I'm not that Kaede, and it hurts.

It hurts when I see them looking for her.

I'm going to move.

To another city. A place called Fujisawa.

Sakuta said it's close to Enoshima.

We're getting ready to move today.

Sakuta said I should choose what I want to bring.

I don't know what to do with the things in Kaede's room.

The bed and desk and cushions are cute. I like them, but I just can't ever feel like it's my room with them around.

I decided to only take the books and bookshelf.

There are a lot of books by the same author as the novel Sakuta bought me. I want to read them.

Kaede's book collection. There's a lot of them.

Nasuno's coming with us!

We're at the new house.

I have a new room.

The bed, desk, cushion, and curtains are all things I picked looking at a catalog with Sakuta. He got them all for me.

I've decided this is where I'm going to become the best little sister.

I'm going to try to become Sakuta's little sister for real.

I don't know how long that will take.

I think I'll get better eventually.

And getting better means Kaede will come back.

It was Sakuta who made me the Kaede I am. So in this new house, I'm going to be the best little sister I can be, for him.

*   *   *

Sakuta will be a high school student in the spring.

He's going to a place called Minegahara High.

He said you can see the ocean from the school windows.

I would like to go see it.

But I'm afraid to go outside.

I feel like everyone is mad at me for not being old Kaede, and it's scary.

Being looked at like I'm a fake is scary.

Can I not just be me?

Sakuta made dinner.

It was not very good.

But I said it was tasty anyway.

Sakuta said, "This is awful!"

Sakuta's getting better at cooking.

He's improving so fast, you can almost hear him whizzing by.

He said the secret is to follow the recipe.

Sakuta got a job.

He comes home very late now.

It's lonely, but Nasuno and I can guard the house together.

Sakuta used his first paycheck to buy a DVD about pandas.

Pandas are great. They make everything better.

Sakuta brought a professional home with him.

I'm trying to be an understanding sister and close my eyes to these things.

She was very pretty.

*   *   *

Sakuta has a girlfriend now!

I don't believe it!

But it's true!

I still don't believe it!

It's the professional—I mean, the girl from the other day. Her name is Mai Sakurajima.

She's even prettier than I thought.

I'm worried she's tricking him.

I read a book about honey traps, and I'm very worried.

Mai is really nice.

She's on TV and very popular.

That's amazing. I could never do that.

She's really amazing.

She gave me some clothes.

Sakuta's friend is staying with us now.

Rio Futaba.

She has very big boobs.

I wish she'd lend me some.

Rio says she wishes she could be tall like I am.

Can we trade?

I am too tall for a little sister.

Sakuta has become a delinquent!

Actually, that was a misunderstanding.

Nodoka is Mai's little sister.

She is very sparkly.

A real idol!

She's very nice to me.

*   *   *

I have lots of dreams these days.

Dreams in which I'm little and playing with little Sakuta.

Drawing pictures, playing house.

But I didn't do these things.

I've never been little.

I only know big Sakuta.

I know one thing for sure.

Sakuta regrets a lot of things.

About the other Kaede.

He regrets not being able to help her when she was suffering and being bullied.

He never told me about this, but I can tell.

If I were to vanish, I know he would have regrets. He would feel like he hadn't done anything for me.

So I've made a lot of goals.

Goals the two of us can accomplish together.

I don't want him to regret it if I'm gone.

I want him to be proud that he made my dreams come true.

I want to leave him with lots of fun, happy, laugh-filled memories. Not sad ones.

I'd like it if he could remember me with a smile even when I'm gone.

I'm going to work hard to make that happen.

I have a bruise on my arm.

I've seen this kind of bruise before.

Sakuta is worried, so I hope it heals soon.

Somebody inside me is very scared.

It's like they're crying because they're scared to come out.

But it's okay.
Sakuta is here, and everything will be okay.

The ocean was very big.
The waves were loud!
The *onigiri* Mai made were very good.
Sakuta had fun, too, so I was very happy.
I hope we can all go to the beach again.

I woke up in the hospital.
Apparently, I collapsed all of a sudden and wouldn't wake up.
They did a lot of tests. Apparently, I am healthy.
But Sakuta doesn't look so good.
The way he looks at me is very sad.
I think I don't have much time left.

I'm scared.
I'm dreaming every night.
I know what that means.
These are Kaede's memories.
That's why I'm scared.
I don't know how much longer I can be me.
I don't know if I can put circles by all my goals.
I'm scared I'll leave Sakuta with regrets.

Please.
I just need a bit more time.
I want Sakuta to smile when he remembers me.
I want all his memories to be filled with laughter.
So I just need a little longer.

*   *   *

Thanks to Sakuta, I managed to put victory circles next to lots of things!

With flowers!

I was too scared to go outside, but I can do that now.

We went over to Mai's house.

I rode the train.

We played on the beach.

We had a picnic!

I saw the pandas!

We cheated a bit, but I went to school!

All because Sakuta helped.

Sakuta has made me very happy.

I'm happy I could be Sakuta's little sister.

I love him now, tomorrow, and forever!

Tomorrow we're going to school in daylight.

He couldn't stop the tears from flowing.

Sakuta was curled up in the bathtub, bawling like a little kid.

He had no way of fighting off these feelings.

He was being tossed around by external forces he had no means of contesting.

But he tried to resist anyway.

He turned the shower on, trying to hide the sobs. He stuck his head under the water, trying to wipe the tears away. But they wouldn't stop.

The feelings in his chest just kept swelling up.

The feelings Kaede had left him with. Warm feelings.

"No need to hold it in."

It was Shouko's voice coming from outside the bathroom door.

She could hear his sobbing, even with the shower running.

"You're an idiot, Sakuta."

"I can't cry!" he wailed. His voice was so choked with sobs it was probably not intelligible. Even he wasn't sure what he'd said. "She wouldn't want me to cry here!"

She'd worked hard for this moment.

Done everything she could to leave him with a smile.

She'd set all those goals so he wouldn't regret a thing.

She'd worked so hard to make him into a good brother who looked after his sister.

She'd made him into a great brother, one who made his sister's wishes come true.

Sakuta was certain he wasn't allowed to cry.

"Kaede did so much! I can't ruin it now."

"Yeah, you're right about that," Shouko said.

Her warm voice softly accepting his feelings.

"You make a good point, Sakuta. But right now? You're allowed to cry."

"But Kaede…"

"Like the flower circles in her notebook, this grief is something important that she gave you. It's proof of how much she meant to you."

"!"

"You're her big brother, so you've got to deal with all of it."

Even when Shouko scolded him, she was nice. And there were tears in her voice, too.

"Unh…uagh…ahh…"

Sakuta was still trying to stifle his sobs.

"Ahhh…auughhhhh!"

But he couldn't hold them back any longer.

Shouko's words had struck the soft part of his heart with uncanny accuracy.

Kaede had given him this grief.

It was proof of the two years they'd lived together.

These feelings came from the memories of her seared into his mind.

And nothing that important could be sealed away inside or denied.

"Aughhhhhhhhhhhhh!!"

The shower water slammed against his head so hard it almost hurt. Sakuta threw his head back like a bawling child, crying out loud. Letting his emotions run wild as they pleased.

So that he could go on living with Kaede's memories.

So that one day he could talk about her with a smile.

Remember her with warmth.

Memory after memory of his time with Kaede floated into Sakuta's head, and he cried like a lost child.

7

It felt like there was a cavernous pit in his belly.

Sakuta was woken up the next morning by an unbearable hunger.

His stomach was making very loud noises.

The sounds were so loud they startled him awake.

He put one hand on his empty stomach and sat up.

Another stomach growl echoed across the room.

"Guess I'm hungry," he said. His voice was a rasp. Caught in his throat.

The cause was half extreme starvation and half because he'd cried his eyes out the day before.

He'd gone to bed like that, so his cheeks were covered in dried tears.

He got up to go wash his face. In the mirror over the sink, his eyes were certainly puffy, but otherwise it was his default sleepy expression.

He scrubbed his face with cold water.

That banished the last traces of slumber. His mind was clear again.

He glanced in the mirror once more.

"You look awful," he said aloud. And then laughed. "And you're insanely hungry."

The pit in his belly wasn't a joke. He genuinely felt you could see a depression there. It wasn't often he felt this hungry. This was what a truly empty belly felt like.

And this sensation struck him as funny.

The more time passed, the more he saw the humor in it. He chuckled out loud. His shoulders shook with laughter. He couldn't stop cracking up. The dried tears around his eyes stung.

He didn't want to stop laughing. He couldn't.

No matter how much fun you have, no matter how sad you get, no matter how much you rail against the universe—your emotions don't matter. You still get hungry all the same.

And his body's obliviousness felt really good right now. Sakuta was grateful for it. This reminder of the daily routine had made him remember what laughter felt like. And once he started laughing, things didn't seem to matter so much.

He couldn't dwell on it forever.

When he finally stopped chuckling, he went to the kitchen.

He grabbed a slice of bread and took a huge bite. Didn't stop to toast it or spread any jam or margarine. He just savored the natural sweetness of white bread. It was never something he paid much attention to, but bread *did* have a flavor.

He grabbed a tomato from the fridge and rinsed it off, then bit right into it. Juicy. The liquid passed through his throat, seeping into his dried-out body.

Sakuta ate quickly, rose to his feet, then took a shower and changed into his uniform. It was a weekday. An ordinary Wednesday. There would be classes to attend, just like always.

Shouko had placed three dining room chairs in a row and was curled up on them, sound asleep.

He left a note for her—

Off to school.

—and left the house a full hour early.

He walked alone down the road outside.

The cold morning air felt good.

Like it was purifying his body.

His steps felt light.

Sakuta was not headed to school.

His first stop was the hospital, where Kaede was.

It wasn't visiting hours yet, but when he stepped up to the nurses' station, someone recognized him and let him in.

He bowed and headed to Kaede's room.

He stopped outside the door and knocked without hesitation.

Twice.

"C-come in!" Kaede said, sounding a bit nervous.

Sakuta opened the door.

"Oh," she said when she saw him. Her jaw dropped.

"Mornin'."

"Oh, right, mornin'."

He shut the door behind him and sat down on a stool by the bed.

"What happened to you yesterday?" Kaede asked.

"Mm?"

"You went to the bathroom and never came back."

"I had the worst diarrhea, and now me and that toilet are best friends for life."

That was the first excuse that crossed his mind. He couldn't exactly tell her the truth.

"Wow, that's gross."

She pulled away from him.

"More importantly, Kaede…"

"What?"

"Do you like pandas?"

"Huh? Where'd that come from?"

"Do you?"

She thought about it. "...I guess so, yeah."

"Then when you get out, we should go see them."

"Fine, but why?"

"I just want to. You should join me."

"Since when do you like pandas?"

Kaede frowned at him. This was new information to her, clearly.

"It's a new thing."

"Huh."

She looked skeptical.

"Aren't you, like, in high school now?"

"High school boys are allowed to like pandas."

"N-not that. I mean...instead of doing things with your sister, shouldn't you have a girlfriend and be taking her on dates?"

The grin that slipped out suggested she was making fun of him.

"I mean, I'll come along. I feel sorry for you, after all."

She was definitely assuming Sakuta didn't have a girlfriend.

"Just to be clear, I *do* have a girlfriend."

".....What?!"

That was a very delayed response.

"You're kidding!!"

"Is it really such a shock?"

"Y-you?! A girlfriend?!"

Apparently, Sakuta getting a girlfriend was a monumental crisis for her. But if she was this surprised already, she was in trouble. *Who* he was dating was going to be a way bigger shock.

"I'll introduce you later. Brace yourself."

Nobody would ever suspect their brother was dating Mai Sakurajima. It would blow her mind.

"I—I can't believe you're seeing someone..."

"We're still stuck on this?"

"I mean…"

Sakuta talked to her until he was in real danger of being late for school. They chatted about nothing in particular, but that was how it should be. That was how family talked. About whatever crossed your mind. Siblings who could do that were doing all right.

They just had to pass the time together, living ordinary lives. Thinking about new Kaede still made him want to cry, but even with that prickling sensation at the back of his nose, he knew he just had to take one day at a time, and he'd get through it.

And something new would grow.

Last
Chapter

chance encounter

The results of an extensive battery of tests showed nothing was physically wrong with Kaede.

But the hospital took their time releasing her.

She was fully conscious and alert, but there was an obvious two-year gap in Kaede's memories. All the time she'd spent as new Kaede was missing.

From her perspective, she'd just woken up one morning to find two whole years had passed. That was a lot to take in, and they decided she'd need some time to adjust to the changes in her life.

She no longer lived in the same town or attended the same school. She'd woken up thinking she was a first-year student, but she was now in her third year of junior high. And near the end of the second term.

There was no way she could just accept all of that, process it, and go back to living like nothing had happened.

The gap between her perceptions and reality was far too vast.

She was even a little uncomfortable being around Sakuta.

"It's like you're a grown-up," she'd said.

They would have to work through each discrepancy. And that couldn't be done overnight.

A week in the hospital would help lay the groundwork.

Sakuta didn't see a reason to argue with that. He swung by the hospital every day after school.

*   *   *

December 1. Monday.

Only one more month left in the year.

When classes finished, Sakuta had some time before his shift at work, so he swung by Kaede's room at the hospital.

He knocked at the door.

"Come in."

When she answered, he slid the door open.

Kaede was sitting on the bed, her back against the wall, her knees up. There was a book resting on her knees—but not a novel.

A notebook. New Kaede's notebook.

When she'd asked about the missing two years, he'd brought it here for her.

She'd been reluctant to look at it that day, but it seemed curiosity had gotten the better of her.

She was pretty absorbed in what was written on those pages.

Sakuta sat down on the stool by the bed. Kaede closed the book. For some reason, she was blushing. She put the notebook down on the bedside table, acting a little flustered.

"Something weird in there?"

What he knew of the contents wouldn't provoke a reaction like this.

"N-no! Not at all," Kaede insisted. Still very red-faced. "Uh, um…"

"Mm?"

"I have an important question for you."

"You do?"

That was oddly formal.

"I-if it's not true, just say so."

"Okay."

"So, um, well…"

Kaede glanced at him.

Then she hugged a pillow to her chest.

"Well? What?"

"D-did I climb into your bed?"

"You did."

"D-don't let me!"

"I mean, you did it of your own accord. No way for me to stop you."

"I didn't! I would never!"

Kaede buried her face in the pillow. Even her ears were red.

"That would be waaaay too mortifying."

She was talking into the pillow.

"I certainly wouldn't recommended it at your age."

"Well, I still *feel* thirteen!"

She peeped out from behind the pillow, glaring at him.

"I think the second you start junior high, you're already too old."

"Hngg…"

Kaede seemed to disagree. Not wanting to touch *that* with a ten-foot pole, Sakuta changed the subject.

"Oh, right, Kano said she wanted to come visit. You up for it?"

He'd called Kotomi Kano yesterday, telling her Kaede's memories had returned. She'd been shocked into silence, but when he explained more, she started crying. Tears of joy.

"Komi?"

"Yep."

"……"

Kaede's eyes locked onto her bedsheets, frowning. Probably thinking about everything that had happened at her last school. How everyone had used social networks, forums, and free messaging apps to say mean things about her. It had been a rough time.

And for her, it didn't seem like all that much time had passed. She'd spent the last two years on break.

So nothing was really resolved.

Even now that Kaede had her memories back, she was avoiding phones. If someone near her used one, she'd turn away. And she still jumped when she heard one ring or vibrate.

Sakuta knew this was a problem Kaede was going to have to overcome. Along with the Adolescence Syndrome.

After a long think, Kaede looked him right in the eye.

"I'd like to meet her," she said.

"I'll tell her that, then."

"M-mm. And also…"

"Mm?"

"W-will you come with me?"

"Yeah, if you're gonna meet up somewhere, I'll tag along."

"Mm."

Looking relieved, she hugged her pillow again.

"Anything else you'd like to do?"

"Like what?"

"Anything after you get outta here."

"Let me see…"

She paused to think, but it didn't take long.

"Oh!" she said. "Er, uh…Sakuta."

Kaede turned to look right at him. He could tell from her eyes how nervous she was.

She took a deep breath.

And then another.

"I want to go to school," she said. "I want that to be possible."

Her eyes shifted from him to the side table. The notebook new Kaede had left for her.

"You're not scared anymore?"

Back in the day, Kaede had constantly said she didn't want to go. Every morning, she'd refuse to get out of bed, hoping the day would just end. But morning always came again, and the cycle of suffering continued.

"I—I think I'll be okay."

The tremor in her voice did not inspire confidence.

But she put her hand on her chest, and he knew what she wanted to say.

"Because I'm not alone," she said with an embarrassed smile. It was a little forced. Putting a brave face on it.

But it made Sakuta feel a bit better.

Like everything was gonna be okay.

They hadn't accomplished anything yet. That was still all ahead of them.

They hadn't even taken the first step. All they'd done was look up.

But there was a warmth in Sakuta's chest.

He was full of the kindness new Kaede had left him.

After seeing Kaede, Sakuta worked his shift, getting back to his apartment around half past nine that night.

It was raining, so he paused outside the door to brush the water off his uniform. It was a mist-like rain, so he hadn't bothered using an umbrella, but now that he actually bothered to check his clothes, he realized he was pretty wet. His hair was dripping, too.

He pulled his key out of his pocket.

"I'm home," he called. The lights were already on—at the entrance, in the hall, and in the living room.

The sound of slippers came down the hall from that brightly lit living room.

"Welcome back!" said an older woman in an apron, with a smile. "Will you have dinner? Or a bath? Or maaaaybe…"

"Are you gonna finally explain what this is?" he asked, interrupting the cliché joke. The question caught in his throat.

The woman in the apron—Shouko—had been staying with him since that fateful day. Shouko Makinohara. If he took her word for it, she was nineteen. "I don't actually have a place to stay. Can you put me up for a while?" she'd said, the day after they were reunited. That Friday evening.

What with Kaede and everything, Sakuta's head was still spinning, so he allowed it. But that and a lot of other details had wound up on the back burner until now.

And Kaede was definitely one reason for that. Sakuta just hadn't been able to focus on anything else all weekend, so here they were, on Monday.

But the other reason was because every time he asked, Shouko deflected.

He'd asked the same question the day before, and she'd said, "Time for my bath!" and pushed him away. And when she'd gotten out, she said, "Staying up late is bad for your skin! Good night!" and gone right to bed.

"Teenage girls need our secrets," she said, clearly hell-bent on wriggling out of it once again.

"Teenage? Shouko, you're basically an adult now. I think you've grown out of secrets."

She definitely seemed way more mature than he remembered her. She'd gone from a high school girl to a college girl.

"I'm risking a lot letting you stay here, you know."

If Mai found out about this, there was no telling what she'd say. The only reason they hadn't already been caught was because Mai was on location, filming. Away from home for ten whole days. But that wouldn't last forever. On the phone last night, she'd said she only had three more days to go.

Which meant that was his time limit.

He had to do something about this situation before Mai got back. At the very least, he wanted to arm himself with the information needed to explain it.

Who *was* Shouko? Her connection to the junior high Shouko remained a mystery. He'd tried calling the younger one two days ago, but she hadn't picked up. Or returned his call since then.

"Fine," Shouko said, sighing. "I'll explain, but first, take a bath. This is gonna take a while, and you'll catch a cold if you stand there dripping."

This didn't *sound* like another trick, so he did as she suggested. The cold winter rain had certainly taken its toll on him.

*   *   *

He took a nice long soak.

Until the warmth had dispelled the last of the chill the rain had given him.

Part of him was feeling pretty impatient. He wanted to hop right out and hear Shouko's long story.

The reason he didn't was because he didn't want to seem too eager. That would just put him at her mercy. And she might find another way to worm out of it if he wasn't careful.

That trace of stubbornness, and a bit of a gamble, meant he took a much longer bath than usual. By the time he left, he was thoroughly baked.

His skin was flushed red from the heat. As he dried himself off, he worried that might give her yet another opening.

Worrying about that, he put his underwear on—and the intercom rang.

"Coming!"

A pair of slippers went down the hall outside the changing room. Heading for the door.

But it was past ten. Who could that be at this hour? A delivery? He hadn't ordered anything.

"……"

He had a bad feeling about this.

"No, wait! Shouko!"

He hastily flung open the changing room door. His instincts were screaming that he had to stop Shouko before she opened the front door. Every part of his body yelled "Danger!"

But, well. It was already too late.

The door had swung open.

And Shouko was beckoning someone in with a smile.

"……"

Sakuta's mouth opened to yelp, but no sound came out. He froze halfway out the changing room door, unable to move. Dressed only in boxers, he felt time stop.

There were two girls in front of him. Both older than him. One had been staying with him the last few days—Shouko, still wearing that apron.

And the other was Mai, wearing a sedately colored coat. She had a paper bag in one hand. Likely some souvenirs she'd bought in Kanazawa.

Mai looked him right in the eye and turned on her heel.

"Uh, wait! Mai!" he yelled. But this was the wrong response.

There was a click.

Mai had locked the door. She even put the chain in place. Like she was trapping someone in a cage.

"I thought you were acting funny on the phone the last few days," she said, turning to face them. "So this is why? And here I thought you were all depressed about Kaede. I came home right away because I was worried."

She took her shoes off and stepped up into the apartment.

"Sakuta," she said.

"Y-yes?"

"You're going to explain everything."

"Well, yeah. I'll try."

But the only problem was, he didn't really get it, either. What was going on here?

"What's the word for situations like this?" Shouko asked, like she wasn't a key part of it. "Oh! A crisis!" She clapped her hands, grinning merrily.

It was going to be a long night.

afterword

This is Volume 5 of the *Rascal* series.

The first volume was *Rascal Does Not Dream of Bunny Girl Senpai*, the second was *Rascal Does Not Dream of Petite Devil Kohai*, the third was *Rascal Does Not Dream of Logical Witch*, and the fourth was *Rascal Does Not Dream of Siscon Idol*, so if this volume made you curious, I suggest you pick those up as well.

If you thought this was the first volume...I'm sorry.

I stand beneath the same sky as you, hoping such accidents will soon come to an end.

This series may have reached its fifth volume, but it seems the next work I bring you won't be a novel at all.

The manga adaption by Tsugumi Nanamiya will be starting in *Dengeki G's Comic* soon—please take a look. You'll be able to enjoy Mai from all sorts of perspectives.

And I imagine the bellyband will have more details, but we're doing something related to the series on Nico Nico Douga. I actually know what we're doing, but at the moment of writing, my part in it isn't getting anywhere, so I'm laying down some defenses...

I hope you can enjoy these projects alongside the main novel series.

Once again, I'd like to thank the illustrator, Keji Mizoguchi, and my editors, Araki and Fujiwara, for their joint efforts.

*   *   *

And my greatest thanks to you, my readers, for accompanying me this far.

And as we end all afterwords, I trust we'll meet again in Volume 6.

Hajime Kamoshida